Samuel French Acting Edition

The Freedom of the City
A Play in Two Acts

by Brian Friel

SAMUELFRENCH.COM   SAMUELFRENCH.CO.UK

FOR PRODUCTION ENQUIRIES

UNITED STATES AND CANADA
Info@SamuelFrench.com
1-866-598-8449

UNITED KINGDOM AND EUROPE
Plays@SamuelFrench.co.uk
020-7255-4302

Each title is subject to availability from Samuel French, depending upon country of performance. Please be aware that *THE FREEDOM OF THE CITY* may not be licensed by Samuel French in your territory. Professional and amateur producers should contact the nearest Samuel French office or licensing partner to verify availability.

Please refer to page 83 for further copyright information.

THE FREEDOM OF THE CITY was first presented in the United States at the Goodman Theatre Center, Chicago, Illinois. The director was William Woodman, the setting by David Jenkins, costumes by Alicia Finkel, and lighting by F. Mitchell Dana.

CAST OF CHARACTERS
(In Order of Speaking)

POLICE CONSTABLE .... *Charles W. Noel*

JUDGE .... *Maurice D. Copeland*

DR. DOBBS, *an American Sociologist* .. *David Whitaker*

SKINNER .... *Lenny Baker*

LILY .... *Frances Hyland*

MICHAEL .... *Allan Carlsen*

SOLDIERS .... *Timothy Himes, Ian Williams, Tim Oman*

LIAM O'KELLY, Radio Telefis Eireann
    Commentator .... *Frank Miller*

BARKEEP .... *Charles W. Noel*

BALLADEER .... *Robert Swan*

PRIEST .... *Fred Michaels*

PRESSMEN .... *Timothy Himes, Ian Williams*

ARMY PRESS OFFICER .... *Stephen Parr*

BRIGADIER JOHNSON-HANSBURY .... *Tony Mockus*

DR. WINBOURNE, *Army Forensic Expert* .. *James Miller*

PROFESSOR CUPPLEY, Pathologist ..... *Edward Meekin.*

3

The play was presented at the Alvin Theatre, New York City, by Konrad Matthaei and Hale Matthews on February 17, 1974, with the same director and designers, and the following changes from the Chicago cast:

POLICE CONSTABLE .... *Edward Holmes*

DR. DOBBS .... *Joe Ponazecki*

LILY .... *Kate Reid*

SOLDIERS .... *J. Kenneth Campbell, Reno Roop*

LIAM O'KELLY .... *Gordon Gould*

BARKEEP .... *Howard Honig*

PRIEST .... *Henderson Forsythe*

PRESSMEN .... *Reno Roop, William Bogert*

ARMY PRESS OFFICER .... *J. Kenneth Campbell*

BRIGADIER JOHNSON-HANSBURY ...... *William Bogert*

DR. WINBOURNE .... *Howard Honig*

PROFESSOR CUPPLEY .... *Edward Holmes*

CHARACTERS

LILY is 43. She has 11 children and her body has long since settled into its own comfortable contours. But poverty and child-bearing have not completely obliterated the traces of early prettiness.

SKINNER is 21. Very lean, very tense, very restless. He is described as 'glib' but the adjective is less than just. A quick volatile mind driving a lean body.

MICHAEL is 22. Strong, regular features but not handsome.

PRESS PHOTOGRAPHER

PRIEST

JUDGE

POLICE CONSTABLE

DR. DOBBS—Sociologist

BALLAD SINGER

BRIGADIER JOHNSON HANSBURY

ARMY PRESS OFFICER

DR. WINBOURNE—Forensic expert

PROFESSOR CUPPLEY—Pathologist

LIAM O'KELLY—RTE Commentator

SOLDIERS, REPORTERS, BARKEEP

TIME: 1970

PLACE: Derry City, Northern Ireland.

5

THE SET

The Mayor's parlour in the Guildhall takes up almost the entire stage. However, stage left and behind it is a section of the stone wall which borders Guildhall Square. There is an archway entrance through this wall up left and a short section of buttress and fence extends out from it at the extreme left. The top of the wall has a railing and is obviously accessible as a promenade. There are bits of rubble and barbed wire scattered about.

Down right is a small platform for the Judge. It contains a desk, a swivel chair and a microphone on a stand.

The parlour is on the main floor of a neo-gothic building. One doorway up right leads to a dressing-room off. Another doorway left opens to the exterior. A stained glass window upstage looks out on Guildhall Square and dominates the room.

The furnishings are solid and dated, the atmosphere heavy and staid. The walls and doors of the parlour are oak paneled.

A large desk with a leather covered top and ornate fittings. A glass display cabinet. An old-fashioned radiogram on top of which sits a vase of artificial flowers.

On one side of the door leading to the dressing-room stands a Union Jack flag. On the other side a large portrait of a forgotten civic dignitary.

A grand baroque chair for the Mayor; two upright carved chairs for his guests; an upholstered stool downstage.

In the "fourth wall" right is an imaginary "door" leading to the corridor; left is an imaginary "mirror." These are both indicated by the actors' business, but never touched or mimed.

NOTE: For easy reference the play has been divided into 17 scenes called: 1-A, 1, 2-A, 2, etc., through 9-A. The "A" scenes precede their numbered counterparts and take place outside of the Guildhall. The numbered scenes all deal directly with our three principal characters and take place inside the Mayor's Parlour.

The Freedom of the City

ACT ONE

*As the House Lights go out, we hear a clock tower chime the four quarter-hours, then strike six o'clock. As the stage lights illuminate the apron in cold blue light, we hear the distant wail of an ambulance siren. Three bodies lie grotesquely across the front of the stage—*SKINNER *Stage Left,* LILY *Center,* MICHAEL *Stage Right.*

A PHOTOGRAPHER, *crouching for fear of being shot, runs on from Right and very hastily and very nervously photographs the corpses—*SKINNER *first, then* LILY, *then* MICHAEL. *His flash bulb lights up the stage each time, and a pool of light surrounds each corpse in turn. When he has photographed* MICHAEL, *a* PRIEST *enters Right, crouching like the photographer and holding a white handkerchief above his head. He gets down on his knees beside* MICHAEL *and hastily blesses him and mumbles a prayer in his ear. He then moves on to* LILY *and to* SKINNER *and goes through the same ritual with each in turn during the following scene.*

When the PHOTOGRAPHER *has taken his photo of* LILY, *he exits Up Left. The lights snap on Right and Left, picking up the* JUDGE *at his desk and microphone Right, and a police* CONSTABLE *Left. The* CONSTABLE *is wearing dark glasses and refers to his notebook. The* JUDGE *takes notes. The* JUDGE *is English, in his early sixties; a quick fussy man with a testy manner.*

SCENE 1-A

CONSTABLE. Hegarty, my lord.

JUDGE. Speak up, Constable, please.

CONSTABLE. Hegarty, my lord.

JUDGE. Yes.

POLICEMAN. Michael Joseph. Unmarried. Unemployed. Lived with his parents.

JUDGE. Age?

POLICEMAN. 22 years, my lord.

JUDGE. Was the deceased known to you personally, Constable? (THREE SOLDIERS *in full combat uniform run on from right. Two of them grab* MICHAEL *by the hands and drag him off right while a third, tense and scared, covers them with his rifle. As they move him the pool of light in which he was lying goes out.*)

POLICEMAN. No, my lord.

JUDGE. And when you arrived at the body, did you discover any firearms on his person or adjacent to his person?

POLICEMAN. I wasn't the first to get there, my lord.

JUDGE. Would you answer my question?

POLICEMAN. I personally saw no arms, my lord.

JUDGE. Thank you. (*The* PRIEST *moves to* LILY.)

POLICEMAN. Doherty. Elizabeth. Married. Aged 43 years.

JUDGE. Occupation?

POLICEMAN. Housewife. Also a cleaning woman. Deceased lived with her family in a condemned property behind the old railway—a warehouse that was converted into eight flats and—

JUDGE. We are not conducting a social survey, Constable. Was the deceased known to you? (*A* SOLDIER *returns and drags* LILY *off right by the coat collar. Another covers him as before. Her pool of light goes out.*)

POLICEMAN. No, my lord.

JUDGE. And did you discover any firearms on her person or adjacent to her person?

POLICEMAN. I wasn't the first on the scene, my lord.

JUDGE. I am aware of that, Constable.

POLICEMAN. I saw no weapons, my lord. (*The* PRIEST *moves on to* SKINNER.)

POLICEMAN. Fitzgerald. Adrian Casimir.

JUDGE. Pardon? (*The* SOLDIERS *return; one covers them while the other drags* SKINNER *off up left. The* SOLDIER *with the rifle picks up a ceremonial hat which was lying beside the body. The pool of light goes out. The* PRIEST *follows.*)

POLICEMAN. Fitzgerald—

JUDGE. I've got that.

POLICEMAN. Adrian Casimir.

JUDGE. Yes.

POLICEMAN. Aged 21. Single. No fixed address.

JUDGE. You mean he wasn't native to the city?

POLICEMAN. He was, my lord. But he moved about a lot. And we haven't been able to trace any relatives.

JUDGE. Had the deceased a profession or a trade?

POLICEMAN. No, my lord.

JUDGE. Was he bearing any firearms—when you got to him?

POLICEMAN. Not when I got to him, my lord.

JUDGE. And was he known to you personally, Constable B?

POLICEMAN. Yes, my lord.

JUDGE. As a terrorist?

POLICEMAN. He had been in trouble many times, my lord. Petty larceny, disorderly behaviour—that sort of thing.

JUDGE. I see. Thank you, Constable. (*Lights go out on the* CONSTABLE, *who exits left.*) I should explain that I have permitted soldiers and policemen to give evidence under pseudonyms so that they may not expose themselves to the danger of reprisal. And before we adjourn for lunch, may I repeat once more and make abundantly clear once more my words of this first day: that this tribunal of enquiry, appointed by Her Majesty's govern-

ment, is in no sense a court of justice. Our only function
is to form an objective view of the events which occurred
in the City of Londonderry, Northern Ireland, on the
tenth day of February, 1970, when after a civil rights
meeting British troops opened fire and three civilians lost
their lives. It is essentially a fact-finding exercise; and
our concern and our only concern is with that period of
time when these three people came together, seized possession of a civic building, and openly defied the security
forces. The facts we garner over the coming days may
indicate that the deceased were callous terrorists who had
planned to seize the Guildhall weeks before the events of
February 10; or the facts may indicate that the mis-
guided scheme occurred to them on that very day while
they listened to revolutionary speeches. But whatever conclusion may seem to emerge, it must be understood that
it is none of our function to make moral judgements, and
I would ask the media to bear this in mind. We will
resume at two-thirty. (*He leaves. Lights go out on the*
JUDGE's *platform.*)

(DR. DODDS *walks on from right into a lighted area down
    right, and addresses the audience. An American
    Professor with an informal manner.*)

DODDS. Good evening. My name is Philip Alexander
Dobbs. I'm a sociologist and my field of study is in-
herited poverty or the culture of poverty or more ac-
curately the subculture of poverty. And since I'll be
using these terms off and on, let me explain what I mean
by them. I'm talking about those people who are at the
very bottom of the socio-economic scale and more spe-
cifically about their distinctive way of life—a way of life
which is common to ghetto or slum communities all over
the Western world and which is transmitted from generation to generation. And the first thing to be said about
this culture or way of life is that it has two aspects: it
is an adaptation of the poor to their marginal position

in a class-structured, highly individuated, capitalistic society; and it is also their method of reacting against that society. And once it comes into existence—this way of life, this culture—it tends to perpetuate itself from generation to generation because of its effect on the children. Because by the time children are six or seven they have usually taken on the basic values and attitudes of their subculture and aren't psychologically geared to take advantage of changing conditions or increased opportunities that may occur in their lifetime.

(*Suddenly all sounds are drowned out by the roar of approaching tanks. Their noise is deafening and fills the whole auditorium. They stop and we hear the sounds of a crowd screaming in panic and confusion. Then over this we hear the voice of a woman:—*)

WOMAN'S VOICE. Stand your ground! Don't move! Don't panic! This is your city! This is your city! (*The sound of the crowd subsides a bit and we realize that* DODDS *has been speaking through all of this, quite oblivious to it all:—*)

DODDS. People with a culture of poverty are provincial and locally oriented and have very little sense of history. They know only their own troubles, their own neighbourhood, their own local conditions, their own way of life; but they don't have the knowledge or the vision or the ideology to see that their problems are also the problems of the poor in the ghettos of New York and London and Paris and Dublin—in fact all over the Western world. To give you some examples: they share a hatred of the police and a mistrust of government, and very often a cynicism to the church. And any movement—trade union, religious, civil rights, pacifist, revolutionary—any movement which gives them this objectivity, organizes them, gives them real hope, promotes solidarity, such a movement inevitably destroys the psychological and social core of the mould, even though they may still be desperately poor. (DODDS *goes off right.*)

(*The stage goes dark for an instant. Then there is an explosion off left and the lights come up on the exterior of the Guildhall. There are large quantities of smoke—CS gas—around the wall and archway,* MICHAEL *staggers on stage left. He has been blinded by the gas, can scarcely breathe, and is retching. He blunders against the short section of fence stage left, and tries to climb over it. He hangs there choking. Then* LILY *enters through the archway. She too, is affected by the gas, but not as badly as* MICHAEL. *She holds a handkerchief to her streaming eyes and her free hand is extended in front of her, feeling her way along the arched entrance. An explosion goes off just behind her and she moves away from the arch and downstage.* SKINNER *enters from right at a full run. He has been caught by a water-cannon—the upper half of his body is soaked. He passes the downstage corner of the set, brushes past* LILY *who is next to the fence, and heads upstage for the archway. Another explosion makes him retreat from the archway. He discovers the door into the parlour and flings it open. He glances inside and then calls to* LILY.)

SCENE 1

SKINNER. Hi! Missus! There's a place up here!

LILY. Where?

SKINNER. Up here! Come on! Quick! Quick!

LILY. Give me a hand, young fella. You'll have to lead me. (*He runs down to her, grabs her arm, and drags her roughly upstage.*)

SKINNER. Come on—come on—come on! Move, will you!? Move!

LILY. No need to pull the arm off me.

SKINNER. In here. Quick. Watch the step. Did you get a dose of the CS gas?

LILY. D'you think I'm playing blind-man's-bluff? God,

you're a rough young fella, too. My good coat! Mother of God, will you watch my good coat!

SKINNER. I should have left you to the soldiers.

LILY. They'd be no thicker nor you.

SKINNER. D'you want to go back to them, then?

LILY. Don't be so damned smart.

SKINNER. There's a chair behind you.

LILY. I can manage myself. (*She drops into a chair and covers her face with both hands,* SKINNER *closes the door and starts to lock it.*) O my God, that's sore on the eyes. There's someone else back there.

SKINNER. Where?

LILY. Just outside. (SKINNER *rushes out of the room.*) Where's this, young fella? Whose house is this? (SKINNER *finds* MICHAEL *hanging from the fence and pulls him down.* MICHAEL *falls.*)

SKINNER. Come on! Get up! They're going wild out there! (MICHAEL *groans.*) Are you hurt? Did you get a rubber bullet?

MICHAEL. Gas.

SKINNER. You're okay. Come on. You can't lie here. Can you walk?

MICHAEL. Leave me. (*There is a sudden burst of rubber bullets.* SKINNER *and* MICHAEL *fall flat on their faces until the burst is over. Then* SKINNER *picks him up by the back of the coat and half drags, half carries him up to the door and into the parlour, as several more explosions go off. He drops him in the middle of the room and runs back to the door, closes it and locks it. As they enter,* LILY *uncovers her eyes momentarily.*)

LILY. I just thought it was a young fella. Is he hurted bad? (*After locking the door,* SKINNER *moves around the room, examining it with quick, lithe efficiency.*)

SKINNER. No.

LILY. (*To* MICHAEL.) Did you get a thump of a baton, young fella?

SKINNER. Gas.

LILY. Maybe he got a rubber bullet in the stomach.

SKINNER. Only gas.

LILY. He might be bleeding internal.

SKINNER. Gas! Are you deaf?

LILY. I like to see the blood. As long as you can see the blood there's always hope.

SKINNER. He'll come round.

LILY. I seen a policeman split a young fella with a baton one Saturday evening on Shipquay Street. His head opened like an orange and the blood spurted straight up—you know, like them pictures you see of whales, only it was red. And at twelve Mass the next day who was sitting in the seat in front of me but your man, fresh as a bap, and the neatest wee plaster from here to here, and him as proud of his-self. (MICHAEL *gets himself into a sitting position on the floor.*)

MICHAEL. Aaaaagh.

LILY. Are you alright, young fella?

MICHAEL. I think so.

LILY. (*To* SKINNER.) I was afeared by the way he was twisting, the kidneys was lacerated.

MICHAEL. That's desperate stuff.

LILY. It's a help if you cross your legs and breathe shalla.

MICHAEL. God—that's awful.

LILY. Did you walk into it or what?

MICHAEL. A canister burst right at my feet.

LILY. You should have threw your jacket over it. They come on us very sudden, didn't they?

MICHAEL. I don't know what happened.

LILY. What got into them anyway?

SKINNER. Did no one tell you the march was banned?

LILY. I knew the march was banned.

SKINNER. Did you expect them to give you tea at the end of it?

LILY. I didn't expect them to drive their tanks through us and shoot gas and rubber bullets into us, young fella. It's a mercy to God if no one's hurted. (*To* MICHAEL.) Where were you standing?

MICHAEL. Beside the platform. Just below the speakers.

LILY. I was at the back of the crowd, beside wee Johnny Duffy—you know—the window-cleaner—Johnny the Tumbler—and I'm telling him what the speakers is saying 'cos he hears hardly anything now since he fell off the ladder the last time. And I'm just after telling him "The streets is ours and nobody's going to move us" when I turn round and Jesus, Mary and Joseph, there's this big Saracen right behind me. Of course I took to my heels. And when I look back there's Johnny the Tumbler standing there with his fists in the air and him shouting, "The streets is ours and nobody's going to move us!" And you could hardly see him below the Saracen. Lord, the chairman'll enjoy that. (MICHAEL *leans against the stool down center and breathes deeply.*) Are you better?

MICHAEL. I'm alright.

LILY. Maybe you concussed yourself when you fell. If you feel yourself getting drowsy, shout "Help! Help!"

MICHAEL. I'm fine.

LILY. D'you know what they say? That the CS gas is a sure cure for stuttering. Would you believe that, young fella? That's why Celia Cunningham across from us drags her wee Colm Damien into the thick of every riot from here to Strabane and him not seven till next May. (MICHAEL *coughs again. She offers him a handkerchief.*) Here.

MICHAEL. Thanks.

LILY. Cough hard.

MICHAEL. I'm fine.

LILY. If you don't get it up, it seeps down through the lungs and into the corpuscles.

MICHAEL. I'm over the worst of it.

LILY. Every civil rights march Minnie McLaughlin goes on—she's the floor above me—she wears a miraculous medal pinned on her vest. Swears to God it's better nor a gas-mask. (MACHAEL *chokes again, almost retches.*) Good on you, young fella. Keep it rising. Anyways, last

Wednesday week Minnie got hit on the leg with a rubber bullet and now she pretends she has a limp and the young fellas call her Che Guevara. If God hasn't said it, she'll be looking for a pension from the Dublin crowd. (SKINNER'S *inspection is now complete—and he realizes where he is. He bursts into sudden laughter—a mixture of delight and excitement and malice.*)

SKINNER. Haaaaaaaaah! (*Still laughing, he jumps up on the desk, then down again in pursuit of* LILY *who takes refuge behind the cocktail cabinet.*)

LILY. Jesus, Mary and Joseph!

SKINNER. Haaaaaaah!

LILY. The young fella's a patent lunatic!

SKINNER. Haaaaaaah!

LILY. Keep away from me, young fella! (SKINNER *goes right to her and they do a tug-of-war over the cocktail cabinet.*)

SKINNER. Do you know where you are, Missus?

LILY. Just you lay one finger on me!

SKINNER. Do you know where you're sitting?

LILY. I'm warning you!

SKINNER. Look around—look around—look around. (SKINNER *swings them—*LILY *and the cocktail cabinet—in a full circle.*) Where are you? Where do you find yourself this Saturday afternoon? (*To both.*) Guess—come on—guess—guess—guess. Ten-to-one you'll never hit it. Fifty-to-one. A hundred-to-one.

MICHAEL. Where?

SKINNER. Where, missus, where?

LILY. How would I know?

SKINNER. I'll tell you where you are.

MICHAEL. Where?

SKINNER. You. Are. Inside. The Guildhall.

LILY. We are not!

SKINNER. In fact, you're in the Mayor's parlour.

LILY. You're a liar!

SKINNER. The holy of holies itself!

LILY. Have a bit of sense, young fella. What would we be doing in—

SKINNER. Look around! Look around!

MICHAEL. How did we get in?

SKINNER. By the side door.

MICHAEL. It's always guarded.

SKINNER. The soldiers must have moved into the Square to break up the meeting. (*To* LILY.) When the trouble started you must have run down Guildhall Street.

LILY. How would I know where I run? I followed the crowd.

SKINNER. (*To* MICHAEL.) You did the same.

MICHAEL. After the canister burst I don't know what happened.

LILY. So we just walked in?

SKINNER. By the side door and in here. Into the private parlour of His Worship, the Lord Mayor of Londonderry. (*He flings a cushion in the air.*) Yipeeeeeeee! (LILY *and* MICHAEL *stand gazing around as the lights shift.*)

(*There are now two light areas left and right and in each is a* SOLDIER *with a portable radio unit on his back.*)

SCENE 2-A

SOLDIER No. 1. Blue Star to Eagle. Blue Star to Eagle.

SOLDIER No. 2. Eagle receiving. Come in, Blue Star.

SOLDIER No. 1. The fucking yobos are inside the fucking Guildhall!

SOLDIER No. 2. Jesus!

SOLDIER No. 1. What the fuck am I supposed to do?

SOLDIER No. 2. How did they get in?

SOLDIER No. 1. On fucking roller skates—how would I know!?

SOLDIER No. 2. How many of them?

SOLDIER No. 1. No idea. The side door's wide open.

SOLDIER No. 2. What's your position, Blue Star?

SOLDIER No. 1. Guildhall Street. At the junction of the quay. What am I to do?

SOLDIER No. 2. Hold that position.

SOLDIER No. 1. Fucking great! For how long?

SOLDIER No. 2. Until you're reinforced.

SOLDIER No. 1. Thanks, mate!

SOLDIER No. 2. Do not attempt to enter or engage.

SOLDIER No. 1. Okay.

SOLDIER No. 2. I'll get back to you in a few minutes. (*Their lights go out and they exit.*)

(*A Television newsman, LIAM O'KELLY appears on top of the wall as a cameraman appears below him.*)

O'KELLY. I am standing on the walls overlooking Guildhall Square in Derry where only a short time ago a civil rights meeting, estimated at about three thousand strong, was broken up by a large contingent of police and troops. There are no reports of serious casualties but unconfirmed reports are coming in that a group of about fifty armed gunmen have taken possession of the Guildhall here below me and have barricaded themselves in. If the reports are accurate, and if the Guildhall, regarded by the minority as a symbol of Unionist domination, has fallen into the hands of the Terrorists, both the Security forces and the Stormont government will be acutely embarrassed. Brigadier Johnson-Hansbury who was in charge of today's elaborate security operation has, so far, refused to confirm or deny the report. No comment either from the Chief Superintendent of Derry's Royal Ulster Constabulary. But usually reliable spokesmen from the Bogside insist that the story is accurate, and already small groups are gathering at street corners within the ghetto area to celebrate, as one of them put it to me, "the fall of the Bastille." This is Liam O'Kelly returning you to our studios in Dublin.

(As he finishes, the lights shift and a BARKEEP *enters right.)*

BARKEEP. Oh, you liked that, did you! Well now we've got a special treat for you: Paddy O'Donnel is going to sing for you a song he just composed about our lads down in the Guildhall. Let's give him a warm welcome! Paddy O'Donnel—our wild colonial boy! (PADDY—*the* BALLADIER—*comes reeling on from right. The* BARKEEP *exits and, to the tune of* John Brown's Body *played on an accordion, the* BALLADEER *sings.*)

BALLADEER. (*To the audience.*) Now listen careful— I'll be askin' you all to join in on the chorus. (*Sings.*)
A hundred Irish heroes one February day
Took over Derry's Guildhall, beside old Derry's quay.
They defied the British Army, they defied the R.U.C.
They showed the crumblin' empire what good Irishmen
    could be.
    (*Spoken.*) Here it is now! (*Sung.*)
Three cheers and then three cheers again for Ireland
    one and free.
For civil rights and unity, Tone, Pearse and Connelly.
The Mayor of Derry City is an Irishman once more.
So let's celebrate our victory and let Irish whiskey pour.

The British Army's leader was a gentle English lad.
If he beat the dirty paddies, they might make him a lord.
So he whispered to his Tommies: 'Fix 'em chaps, I'll see
    you right.'
But the lads inside the Guildhall shouted back, 'Come on
    and fight.'
    (*Spoken.*) Sing it now! (*Sung.*)
Three cheers and then three cheers again for Ireland
    one and free.
For civil rights and unity, Tone, Pearse and Connelly.
The Mayor of Derry City is an Irishman once more.
So lets celebrate our victory and let Irish whiskey pour.
    (*Spoken.*) One more time! (*Sung.*)

Three cheers and then three cheers again for Ireland
    one and free.
For civil rights and unity, Tone, Pearse and Connelly.
The Mayor of Derry City is an Irishman once more.
So let's celebrate our victory and let Irish whiskey pour.
(*He bows his way off right as lights shift back to the
interior of the Guildhall.*)

(MICHAEL *begins to move around the parlour silently,
    deferentially.* LILY *stands very still; only her eyes
    move.* SKINNER *watches her closely. Pause.*)

SCENE 2

MICHAEL. Christ Almighty—the mayor's parlour! (*Silence.*) I was here once before. I don't mean in here—in
his public office—the one down the corridor. Three years
ago—that bad winter—they were taking on extra men to
clear away the snow, and my father said maybe if I went
straight to the top and asked himself . . . That public
office, it's nice enough. But, my God, this . . . (*Silence.*)
    LILY. We shouldn't be here.
    MICHAEL. God, it's very impressive.
    LILY. No place for us.
    MICHAEL. God, it's beautiful, isn't it?
    SKINNER. (*To* LILY.) Isn't it beautiful? (LILY *still
has not moved. She points.*)
    LILY. What's that?
    SKINNER. Record player and radio.
    LILY. And that?
    SKINNER. Cocktail cabinet. What'll you have, Missus?
    LILY. What's in that yoke? (SKINNER *tries to open the
top of the display cabinet.*)
    SKINNER. Locked. But we'll soon fix that. (*He pro-
duces a penknife and deftly forces the lock.*)
    MICHAEL. Feel the door handles. Real oak. And brass.
And feel the walls. The very best of stuff. (SKINNER *takes

out a ceremonial sword and an ancient pistol, each with a descriptive brass label attached.)

SKINNER. This is a "14th Century ceremonial sword with jewelled handle and silver tip." How are you off for swords, Missus?

MICHAEL. Feel the carpet. Like a mattress.

SKINNER. And this is a "Pistol used by Williamite garrison besieged by Jacobite army. 1691."

LILY. Who's that?

SKINNER. (*Reads.*) Sir Joshua Hetherington, M.B.E., V.M.H., S.H.I.T. Is he a mate of yours?

LILY. I was thinking it wasn't the Sacred Heart. (MICHAEL *holds out the cigaret box from the desk.*)

MICHAEL. Feel the weight of that—pure silver. And look—look—real leather—run your hand over it. (*Desk top.*)

SKINNER. We'll have to sign the Distinguished Visitors' Book, Missus. Are you distinguished?

LILY. What's in there? (MICHAEL, *awe-stricken, backs out of the dressing room.*)

MICHAEL. Wardrobes — toilet — wash-hand basin — shower. Pink and black tiles all round. And the taps are gold and made like fishes' heads. (*Closes door.*) God, it's very impressive. Isn't it impressive, Missus?

SKINNER. Isn't it, Missus?

LILY. It's alright.

SKINNER. Two pounds deposit against breakages and it's yours for ten bob a week. Or maybe you don't like the locality, Missus?

LILY. Mrs. Doherty's the name, young fella, Mrs. Lily Doherty.

SKINNER. Are you not impressed, Lily? (MICHAEL *reads the inscription below the stained-glass window.*)

MICHAEL. "Presented to the citizens of Londonderry by the Honourable The Irish Society to commemorate the visit of King Edward VII, July, 1903."

SKINNER. That's our window, Lily. How would it look in your parlour?

MICHAEL. I read about the Honourable The Irish Society. They're big London businessmen and big bankers and they own most of the ground in the city.

LILY. This room's bigger than my whole place.

SKINNER. Have you no gold taps and tiled walls?

LILY. There's one tap and one toilet below in the yard —-and they're for eight families.

SKINNER. By God, you'll sign no distinguished visitors' book, Lily.

LILY. And I'll tell you something, glib boy: if this place was mine, I'd soon cover them ugly bare boards . . . (*The oak walls.*) . . . with nice pink gloss paint that you could wash the dirt off, and I'd put decent glass you could see through into them gloomy windows, and I'd shift Joe Stalin there . . . (*Sir Joshua.*) . . . and I'd put a nice flight of them brass ducks up along that wall. (SKINNER *and* MICHAEL *both laugh.*)

SKINNER. You're a woman of taste, Lily Doherty.

LILY. And since this is my first time here and since you . . . (Skinner) . . . seem to be the caretaker, the least you might do is offer a drink to a ratepayer. (*She sits—taking possession.* MICHAEL *laughs.*)

MICHAEL. The Mayor's parlour—God Almighty!

LILY. (*To* MICHAEL.) And will you quit creeping about, young fella, as if you were doing the Stations of the Cross.

MICHAEL. I never thought I'd be in here.

LILY. Well, now you are. Sit down and stop trembling like Gavigan's greyhound.

SKINNER. What'll you have, Lily?

LILY. What have you got?

SKINNER. Whiskey — gin — rum — sherry — brandy — vodka—

MICHAEL. Ah now, hold on.

SKINNER. What?

MICHAEL. Do you think you should?

SKINNER. What?

MICHAEL. Touch any of that stuff.

SKINNER. Why not?

MICHAEL. Well, I mean to say, it's not ours and we weren't invited here and—

LILY. Lookat, young fella: since it was the British troops driv me off my own streets and deprived me of my sight and vision for a good quarter of an hour the least the corporation can do is placate me with one wee drink. (*Grandly, to* SKINNER.) I think I favour a little port wine, young fella, if you insist. (MICHAEL *comes out of the dressing room giggling—a bit hysterically.*)

MICHAEL. Honest to God, this is mad, really mad—sitting in the Mayor's parlour on a Saturday afternoon—bloody mad.

LILY. What do they call you, young fella?

MICHAEL. Michael.

LILY. Michael what?

MICHAEL. Michael Hegarty.

LILY. What Hegarty are you?

MICHAEL. I'm from the Brandywell.

LILY. Jack Hegarty's son?

MICHAEL. Tommy. My father used to be in the slaughter-house—before it closed down.

LILY. Are you working?

MICHAEL. I was a clerk with a building contractor but he went bust six months ago. And before that I was an assistant storeman in the distillery but then they were taken over. And now my father's trying to get me into the gas-works. My father and the foreman's mates. And in the meantime, I'm going to the tec. four nights a week—you know—to improve myself. I'm doing economics and business administration and computer science.

LILY. You must be smart, young fella.

MICHAEL. I don't know about that. But I'm a lot luckier than my father was. And since that North Sea discovery there's a big future in gas. They can't even guess how big the industry's going to grow.

SKINNER. But you'll be ready to meet the challenge; wise man. Are you smart, Lily?

LILY. Me? I never could do nothing right at school except carry round the roll books. And when the inspector would come they used to lock me in the cloakroom with the Mad Mulligans. Lucky for my wanes the chairman's got the brains.

SKINNER. Mr. Hegarty?

MICHAEL. What?

SKINNER. A drink.

MICHAEL. I don't think I should. I think—

SKINNER. Suit yourself.

LILY. (*To* MICHAEL.) Are you a victim?

MICHAEL. What?

LILY. To the drink.

MICHAEL. No, no, no. It's just that there's no one here and it's not ours and—

LILY. Will you take one drink and don't be such an aul woman! (*To* SKINNER.) Give him a drink, young fella.

MICHAEL. A very small whiskey then.

LILY. Michael's a nice name. I have a Michael. He's seven. Next to Gloria. She's six. And then Timothy—he's three. And then the baby—he's eleven months—Mark Anthony. Everyone of them sound of mind and limb, thanks be to God. And that includes our Declan—he's nine—though he's not as forward as the others—you know—not much for mixing; a wee bit quiet—you know —nothing more nor shyness and sure he'll soon grow out of that, won't he? They all say Declan's the pet. And praise be to Almighty God, not one of them has the chairman's chest. D'you see his chest, young fella? Ask him to carry the water or the coal up the three flights from the yard and you'd think Hurricane Debbie was coming at you. And give him just wan whiff of the stuff we got the day and before you'd blink he'd be life everlasting.

MICHAEL. Five children?

LILY. Five? God look to your wit! Eleven, young fella.

Eight boys and three girls. And they come like a pattern on wallpaper: two boys, a girl, two boys, a girl, two boys, a girl, two boys. If I had have made the dozen, it would have been a wee girl, wouldn't it?

MICHAEL. I—I—it—

LILY. And I would have called her Jasmine—that a gorgeous yalla flower—I seen it once in a wreath up in the cemetery the day they buried Andy Boyle's wife. But after Mark Anthony the chairman hadn't a puff left in him. (SKINNER *hands round the drinks.*)

SKINNER. Compliments of the city.

LILY. Hi! What happened to you?

SKINNER. Me?

LILY. Your hair—your shirt—you're soaked!

SKINNER. The water-cannon got me.

LILY. Will you take that off you, young fella, before you die of internal pneumonia.

SKINNER. I'm dry now.

LILY. Take off that shirt.

SKINNER. I'm telling you—I'm dried out.

LILY. Come here to me.

SKINNER. I'm dry enough.

LILY. I said come here! (*She unbuttons his shirt and takes it off—he is wearing nothing underneath—and dries his hair with it.*)

"Wet feet or a wet chemise
 The sure way to an early demise."

Lord, there's not a pick on him.

SKINNER. Leave me alone. I'm okay.

LILY. And you've been running about like that for the past half hour! What way's your shoes? Are them gutties dry?

SKINNER. I'm telling you—I'm alright.

LILY. Take them off. Take them off. (*He takes off the canvas shoes. He is not wearing socks.*) Give them to me. (*She hangs the shirt on the Mayor's chair, and the shoes too on the finials either side.*) D'you see our Kevin? He's like him (Skinner.) Eats like a bishop and nothing to

show for it. I be affronted when he goes with his class
to the swimming pool.

MICHAEL. Well. To civil rights.

LILY. Good luck, young fella.

SKINNER. Good luck.

MICHAEL. To another great turnout today.

LILY. Great.

MICHAEL. Good luck.

*(The lights shift to the battlements above them where the
    PRIEST appears in a surplice. He addresses a con-
    gregation below him.)*

SCENE 3-A

PRIEST. At eleven o'clock tomorrow morning solemn
requiem Mass will be celebrated in this church for the
repose of the souls of the three people whose death has
plunged this parish into a deep and numbing grief. As
you are probably aware, I had the privilege of administering the last rites to them and the knowledge that they
didn't go unfortified before their Maker is a consolation
to all of us. But it is natural that we should mourn.
Blessed are they that mourn, says our Divine Lord. But
it is also right and fitting that this tragic happening
should make us sit back and take stock and ask ourselves
the very pertinent question: Why did they die?

I believe the answer to that question is this. They died
for their beliefs. They died for their fellow citizens. They
died because they could endure no longer the injuries
and injustices and indignities that have been their lot
for too many years. They sacrificed their lives so that
you and I and thousands like us might be rid of that
iniquitous yoke and might inherit a decent way of life.
And if that is not heroic virtue, then the world sanctity
has no meaning.

No sacrifice is ever in vain. But its value can be di-

minished if it doesn't fire our imagination, stiffen our
resolution, and make us even more determined to see
that the dream they dreamed is realized. May we be
worthy of that dream, of their trust. May we have the
courage to implement their noble hopes. May we have
God's strength to carry on where they left off. In the
name of the Father, Son, and Holy Spirit.

*(As he finishes, the stage goes to black, and from all
sides we hear shocked voices.)*

VOICE No. 1. There's at least a dozen dead.
VOICE No. 2. Where?
VOICE No. 1. Inside the Guildhall.
VOICE No. 3. I heard fifteen or sixteen
VOICE No. 1. Maybe twenty.
VOICE No. 3. And a baby in a pram.
VOICE No. 1. And an old man. They blew his head off.
VOICE No. 2. Oh my God.
VOICE No. 3. They just broke the windows and lobbed
in hand-grenades.
VOICE No. 2. Oh my God.
VOICE No. 1. Blew most of them to smithereens.
VOICE No. 2. Fuck them anyway! Fuck them! Fuck
them! Fuck them!

*(During the above, an area of light has come slowly on
down right revealing O'KELLY and two other RE-
PORTERS. Now a similar area snaps on down left
into which steps an Army PRESS OFFICER.)*

OFFICER. At approximately 15.20 hours today a band
of terrorists took possession of a portion of the Guildhall.
They gained access during a civil disturbance by forc-
ing a side door in Guildhall Street. It is estimated that
up to forty persons are involved. In the disturbance two
soldiers were hit by stones and one by a bottle. There are
no reports of civilian injuries. The area is now quiet and

the security forces have the situation in hand. No further statement will be issued. (*The* REPORTERS *ask their questions with great rapidity.*)

O'KELLY. What portion of the Guildhall is occupied?

OFFICER. The entire first floor.

REPORT NO. 1. Is it true that there are women in there too?

OFFICER. Our information is that women are involved.

REPORTER No. 2. Are they armed?

OFFICER. Our information is that they have access to arms.

REPORTER No. 2. They brought the arms with them or the arms are in there?

OFFICER. We understand that arms are accessible to them.

O'KELLY. What troops and equipment have you brought up?

OFFICER. I cannot answer that.

REPORTER No. 1. Have you been in touch with them?

OFFICER. No.

REPORTER No. 2. Are you going to get in touch with them?

OFFICER. Perhaps.

O'KELLY. Are you going to negotiate with them or are you going to go in after them?

OFFICER. Sorry. That's all I can say.

O'KELLY. When are you going in after them?

REPORTER No. 1. Is it a police or an army operation?

OFFICER. Sorry.

REPORTER No. 2. Why wasn't the Guildhall guarded?

O'KELLY. Who's in charge of ground forces?

REPORTER No. 1. Do you expect a reaction from the Bogside?

OFFICER. Sorry, gentlemen. (*He turns and leaves.*)

(*The* REPORTERS *also turn and leave, muttering. The lights shift back to the parlour.*)

SCENE 3

MICHAEL. It was a big turnout, wasn't it?

LILY. Terrible big.

MICHAEL. And the speeches were good too.

LILY. I don't care much for speeches. Isn't that a shocking thing to say? I can't concentrate—you know?

MICHAEL. They'll never learn, you know; never. All they had to do was sit back nice and quiet; let the speeches be made; let the crowd go home. There wouldn't be no trouble of any kind. But they have to bull in. And d'you know what they're doing? As a matter of fact, they're doing two things: they're bringing more and more people out on the streets—that's fine; but they're also giving the hooligan element an excuse to retaliate—and that's where the danger lies. (SKINNER sneezes—twice.)

LILY. (To SKINNER.) It's a hot whiskey you should be drinking.

MICHAEL. I've been on every civil rights march from the very beginning—right from October 5. And I can tell you there wasn't the thousands then that there was the day. I've even went on civil rights marches that I was far from satisfied about the people that was running them; for as you know as well as me there's a lot of strange characters knuckled in on the act that didn't give a shit about real civil rights—if you'll excuse me, Missus.

LILY. Port wine's gorgeous.

SKINNER. It's sherry, Lily.

MICHAEL. But as I say to Norah, the main thing is to keep a united front. The ultimate objectives we're all striving for is more important than the personalities or the politics of the individuals concerned.

SKINNER. At this point in time.

MICHAEL. What's that?

SKINNER. And taking full cognizance of all relative facts.

MICHAEL. What d'you mean?

LILY. Who's Norah, young fella?

MICHAEL. The girl I'm engaged to.

LILY. (*To* SKINNER.) Ah! He's engaged. (*She goes to the sherry bottle on the desk and pours herself another.*) Congratulations.

MICHAEL. Thanks.

LILY. I wish you health, wealth and every happiness, young fella, and may no burden come your way that you're not fit to carry.

MICHAEL. Thank you.

LILY. When are you getting married?

MICHAEL. Easter.

LILY. (*To* SKINNER.) Easter! I was married at Easter —April 3—my seventeenth birthday. And we spent our honeymoon with the chairman's Auntie Maggie and Uncle Ned in Preston, Lancashire, England, and we seen the docks and everything.

MICHAEL. We're getting married on Easter Tuesday.

LILY. And where will you live?

MICHAEL. We'll live with my people till we get a place of our own.

LILY. (*To* SKINNER.) A place of their own!

SKINNER. Leely, the language I speak a leetle too—yes?

LILY. Norah's a nice name. If the chairman would have had his way, we'd have had a Norah. But I always favoured a Noelle. She's fourteen now. Between Tom and the twins. Born on a roasting August bank holiday Monday at twenty to three in the afternoon, but I called her Noelle all the same.

MICHAEL. (*To* SKINNER.) How many would you say was there today?

SKINNER. No idea.

MICHAEL. Six thousand? More? (SKINNER *shrugs indifferently. He's engrossed in a racing form he has pulled from his pocket.* LILY *sits and removes her shoes; rubs her feet.*) I'm getting pretty accurate at assessing a crowd and my estimate would be between six and six and a half. When the ones at the front were down at the Brandywell, the last of them were leaving the Creggan. I could see both ways 'cos I was in the middle. And the hooligan elements kept well out of the way. It was a good disciplined responsible march. And that's what we must show them—that we're responsible and respectable; and they'll come to respect what we're campaigning for.

LILY. D'you see them shoes? Five pounds in Woolworths and never a day's content since I got them.

MICHAEL. Do you go on all the marches, Lily?

LILY. Most of them. It's the only exercise I get.

MICHAEL. Do you have the feeling they're not as—I don't know—as dignified as they used to be? Like, d'you remember in the early days, they wouldn't let you carry a placard—wouldn't even let you talk, for God's sake. And that was really impressive—all those people marching along in silence, rich and poor, high and low, doctors, accountants, plumbers, teachers, bricklayers—all shoulder to shoulder—knowing that what they wanted was their rights and knowing that because it was their rights nothing in the world was going to stop them getting them.

SKINNER. Shit—if you'll excuse me, Missus. Who's for more municipal booze? (*He refills his own glass and* LILY'S.)

MICHAEL. What do you mean?

SKINNER. It's on the dignified public.

MICHAEL. (*To* LILY.) What the hell does he mean?

LILY. That's enough, Easy—easy.

SKINNER. It's coming off a fine broad back. Another whiskey, Mr. Hegarty?

MICHAEL. Are you for civil rights at all?

SKINNER. 'Course I am. I'm crazy about them. A little drop?

MICHAEL. Not for me.

SKINNER. Just a nip?

MICHAEL. I'm finished.

SKINNER. Have a cigar.

MICHAEL. No.

SKINNER. A cigarette, then.

MICHAEL. No.

SKINNER. Or what about a shower under the golden fish? (LILY *gives a great whoop of laughter*.)

LILY. Haaaaa! A shower! God, but you're a comic, young fella. (SKINNER *lights a cigar and carries his glass to the phone*.)

MICHAEL. I see nothing funny in that.

LILY. D'you see, if it was a Sunday I'd take a shower myself. Sunday's my day. We all have our days for bathing over at the granny's—that's the chairman's mother. She has us all up on a timetable on the kitchen wall, and if you miss your night you lose your turn.

SKINNER. (*Phone.*) Jackie? Yes, it's me. No, as a matter of fact, I'm stripped to the waist and drinking brandy in the mayor's parlour. (*To* LILY *and* MICHAEL.) He's killing himself laughing! (*Into phone*.) Look, Jack, would you put half-a-note on Bunny Rabbit in the 4.30? Decent man. See you tonight. 'Bye.

LILY. I'm glad you've a nice cushy career.

SKINNER. It's not all sunshine, Lily.

LILY. D'you bet heavy?

SKINNER. When I have it.

LILY. That'll be often. What do they call you, young fella?

SKINNER. Skinner.

LILY. Mister Skinner or Skinner what?

SKINNER. Just Skinner.

LILY. Would you be anything to Paddy Skinner that used to keep the goats behind the Mormon chapel?

SKINNER. Both my parents died when I was a baby. I was reared by an aunt. Next question?

LILY. Lord, I'm sorry, son. (*To* MICHAEL.) Both his parents! Shocking. 'Life is not a bed of roses. Sorrow is our daily lot.' (*Suddenly bright*.) But I'll bet you're musical like all the others.

SKINNER. Who?

LILY. Sure, it's well known that all wee orphans is always musical. Orphans can play instruments before they can talk. There was the poor wee Mulherns opposite us —the father and mother both submitted to TB within three days of each other—and when you'd pass that house at night—the music coming out of it—honest to God, you'd think it was the Palais de Dance.

SKINNER. I can play the radio, Lily.

LILY. What's that?

SKINNER. Four ways—loud and soft and off . . . (*He crosses and turns the radio on.*) and on. Can you? (*Waltz music on the radio.*)

LILY. Oh, you're great.

SKINNER. And I play the horses and the dogs.

LILY. You're brilliant.

SKINNER. Thanks.

LILY. Are you working?

SKINNER. No.

LILY. Did you ever work?

SKINNER. For a while when I was at grammar school— before they kicked me out.

LILY. What did you ever do since?

SKINNER. Three years ago I did some potato picking.

LILY. (*To* MICHAEL.) He has a long memory.

SKINNER. And last August I was a conductor on the buses.

LILY. But travel didn't agree with you.

SKINNER. Listen, Lily—isn't that the B.B.C. Orphans Orchestra?

LILY. I'll tell you something—you never had to study glibness. Oh, nothing sharpens the wits like idleness. (*To* MICHAEL.) You stick to your books, son. That's what I say to our boys.

SKINNER. I'll bet you the chairman's glib, Lily.

LILY. The chairman never worked on account of his health. (SKINNER *sings with the radio and does a parody-waltz off and into the dressing-room.*)

SKINNER. 1-2-3; 1-2-3; 1-2-3; 1-2-3.

LILY. (*Calls.*) And he has more brains than you and a dozen like you put together! Brat! Put that thing out!

(MICHAEL *switches radio off.*) Cheeky young brat, that Skinner! Easy seen he never had no mother to tan his backside.

MICHAEL. Was he on the march at all?

LILY. Who?

MICHAEL. Skinner.

LILY. How would I know?

MICHAEL. My suspicion is he just turned up for the meeting.

LILY. The chairman worked for a full year after we married. In Thompson's foundry. But the fumes destroyed the tissues of his lungs. D'you think he likes sitting at the fire all day, reading the wanes' comics?

MICHAEL. That Skinner's a trouble-maker.

LILY. But for all he got no education he's a damn-side smarter nor that buck.

MICHAEL. That's what I was talking about earlier, Lily. Characters like that need watching.

LILY. Who?

MICHAEL. Him.

LILY. What about him?

MICHAEL. I have a feeling about him. I wouldn't be surprised if he was a revolutionary.

LILY. What do they call you again, young fella?

MICHAEL. Michael.

LILY. Michael's a nice name. I have a Michael. He'll be eight next October. You stick to you books, son.

MICHAEL. We'll watch him, Lily. I'm uneasy about that fella.

SCENE 4-A

The lights come up on the judge's platform and a small area down center which BRIGADIER JOHNSON-HANS-BURY *walks into from up left.*

JUDGE. Brigadier Johnson-Hansbury, you were in charge of security on that day.

BRIGADIER. That is correct, my lord.

JUDGE. Could you tell us what strength was at your disposal?

BRIGADIER. The 8th Infantry Brigade, 1st Battalion Parachute Regiment, 1st Battalion Kings Own Border Regiment, two companies of the 3rd Battalion of the Royal Regiment of Fusiliers.

JUDGE. And equipment?

BRIGADIER. Twelve Saracens, ten Saladins, two dozen Ferrets and four water-cannon and a modicum of air-cover.

JUDGE. And the Royal Ulster Constabulary and the Ulster Defence Regiment?

BRIGADIER. They were present, my lord.

JUDGE. Under your command?

BRIGADIER. As a civilian authority.

JUDGE. Under your command?

BRIGADIER. Under my command.

JUDGE. I'm an old army man myself, Brigadier, and it does seem a rather formidable array to line up against three terrorists, however well armed they could have been.

BRIGADIER. At that point we had no idea how many gunmen were inside the Guildhall. Our first reports indicated forty.

JUDGE. But those reports were inaccurate.

BRIGADIER. They were, my lord. But I would like to point out what we were in an exposed position between the terrorists inside the Guildhall and the no-go Bogside areas at our flank and back.

JUDGE. I see. And you, personally, gave the command over the loud-hailer to the terrorists inside to surrender?

BRIGADIER. I did, my lord. On two occasions.

JUDGE. And approximately ten minutes after the second occasion, they emerged?

BRIGADIER. That is correct.

JUDGE. Brigadier, a persistent suggestion keeps cropping up in the various reports about the events of that day and indeed it was voiced strenuously by Counsel for the deceased within these very walls, and I would like to have your reaction to it. The suggestion is that no attempt was made to arrest these people as they emerged, but that they were dealt with 'punitively' as it has been phrased 'to teach the ghettos a lesson.'

BRIGADIER. My lord, they emerged firing from the Guildhall. There was no possibility whatever of effecting an arrest operation. And at that point we understood they were the advance group of a much larger force.

JUDGE. So you dismiss the suggestion?

BRIGADIER. Completely, my lord.

JUDGE. And an arrest was not attempted?

BRIGADIER. Because it wasn't possible in the circumstances.

JUDGE. And had you known, as you learned later, Brigadier, that there were only three terrorists involved, would you have acted differently?

BRIGADIER. My orders would have been the same, my lord.

JUDGE. Thank you, Brigadier.

(The lights shift to DOBBS. The BRIGADIER marches smarty off; The JUDGE turns upstage.)

DOBBS. If you are born into the subculture of poverty, what do you inherit? Well, you inherit an economic condition, and you inherit a social and psychological condition. The economic characteristics include wretched housing, a constant struggle for survival, a chronic shortage of cash, persistent unemployment, and very often real hunger or at least malnutrition. You also inherit a lack of impulse control, a strong present-time orientation with very little ability to defer gratification and to plan for the future, and a sense of resignation and frustration. The reason for this sense of defeat is the existence of a set of values in the dominant class which stresses the accumulation of wealth and property, the desirability of 'improvement' and explains low economic status as a result of personal inadequacy or inferiority.

Middle-class people—with deference people like you and me—we tend to concentrate on the negative aspects of the culture of poverty. We tend to associate negative values to such traits as present-time orientation, and concrete versus abstract orientation. Now, I don't want to idealize or romanticize the culture of poverty; as someone has said, "It's easier to praise poverty than to live in it." But there are some positive aspects which we cannot overlook completely. Living in the present, for example, may develop a capacity for adventure and for spontaneity, for the enjoyment of the sensual, for the indulgence of impulse; and these aptitudes are often blunted or muted in the middle-class, future-oriented man. So that to live in the culture of poverty is, in a sense, to live with the reality of the moment—in other words, to practise a sort of existentialism. The result is that people with a culture of poverty suffer much less from repression than we of the middle-class suffer and indeed, if I may make the suggestion with due qualification, they often have a hell of a lot more fun than we have. Thank you. (DOBBS *goes off left as lights shift back to the parlour.*)

(*The dressing room door is flung open and we see the back of the red cloaked figure emerge.* MICHAEL *utters an exclamation and* LILY *dashes for the door. The figure turns and it's* SKINNER, *dressed in a splendid mayoral robe and chain with a ceremonial hat on his head. At the door:*)

SCENE 4

SKINNER. "You're much deceived; in nothing am I changed/But in my garments!" (*He strikes a pose;* LILY *gives one of her whoops—of relief.*)

LILY. O Jesus, Mary and Joseph!

SKINNER. "Through tattered clothes small vices do appear/Robes and furred gowns hide all.'"

LILY. Mother of God, would you look at him! And the hat! What's the rig, Skinner? (SKINNER *distributes the gowns.*)

SKINNER. Mayor's robes, alderman's robes, councillor's robes. Put them on and I'll give you both the freedom of the city.

LILY. Skinner, you're an eejit!

SKINNER. The ceremomy begins in five minutes. The world's press and television are already gathering outside. "Social upheaval in Londonderry. Three gutties become freemen"— Apologies, Mr. Hegarty! "Two gutties." What happened to the orphans orchestra?

MICHAEL. Catch yourself on, Skinner.

LILY. Lord, the weight of them! They'd cover my settee just lovely! (SKINNER *turns on the radio. A military band—they have to shout to be heard above it.*) Put it on for the laugh, young fella.

SKINNER. Don the robes, ladies and gentlemen, and taste real power. (LILY *puts on her robe; as does* MICHAEL, *reluctantly.* SKINNER *takes the flagpole and begins waving the Union Jack through the air.*)

LILY. Lookat-lookat-lookat me, would you!? (*She dances in front of the "mirror."*) Di-do-do-da-doo-da-da. (*Sings.*) "I know she likes me; I know she likes me because she said so. She is my lily of Laguna; she is my lily and my—" Mother of God, if the wanes could see me now!

SKINNER. Or the chairman.

LILY. Oooooops!

SKINNER. Lily, this day I confer on you the freedom of the city of Londonderry. God bless you, my child. And now, Mr. Hegarty, I think we'll make you a life peer. Arise, Lord Michael—of Gas.

LILY. They make you feel great all the same. You feel you could—you could give benediction!

SINNER. Make way—make way for the lord and lady mayor of Derry Colmcille!

LILY. My shoes—my shoes! I can't appear without

my shoes! (*She sits and quickly puts them on.* MICHAEL *sulks in the mayor's chair.* LILY *joins* SKINNER *in a ceremonial parade before imaginary people. They both affect very grand accents. Very fast.*)

SKINNER. How are you? Delighted you could come.

LILY. How do do.

SKINNER. My wife—Lady Elizabeth.

LILY. (*Blows kiss.*) Wonderful people.

SKINNER. Nice of you to turn up.

LILY. My husband and I.

SKINNER. Carry on with the good work.

LILY. Thank you. Thank you.

SKINNER. Splendid job you're doing.

LILY. We're really enjoying ourselves. (SKINNER *lifts the flowers and hands them to* LILY.)

SKINNER. From the residents of Tintown.

LILY. Oh, my! How sweet! (*Stoops down to kiss a child.*) Thank you, darling. (SKINNER *pauses below Sir Joshua. He is now the stern, practical man of affairs. The accent is dropped.*)

SKINNER. This is the case I was telling you about, Sir Joshua. Eleven children in a two-roomed flat. No toilet, no running water.

LILY. Except what's running down the walls. Haaaaa!

SKINNER. She believes she has a reasonable case for a corporation house.

LILY. It's two houses I need!

SKINNER. Two?

LILY. Isn't there thirteen of us? How do you fit thirteen in one house?

SKINNER. (*To portrait.*) I know. I know. They can't be satisfied.

LILY. Listen! Listen! I know that one! Do you know it, Skinner?

SKINNER. Elizabeth, please.

LILY. It's a military two-step. The chairman was powerful at it. Give us your hand! Come on!

SKINNER. I think you're concussed. (*She drags him into the middle of the parlour and they sing as they dance.*) LILY.

As I walk along the Bois de Boulogne with an independ-
   ent air,
You can hear the girls declare, 'He must be a millionaire'
You can hear them sigh and hope to die and can see them
   wink the other eye
At the man who broke the bank at Monte Carlo.
As I walk along the Bois de Boulogne with an independ-
   dent air,
You can hear the girls declare, 'He must be a millionaire'
You can hear them sigh and hope to die and can see them
   wink the other eye
At the man who broke the bank at MONTE Carlo.
Oh, my God, I'm punctured! (*She collapses on stool down center.*)

SKINNER Lovely, Lily. Lovely.

LILY. I wasn't a bad dancer once.

SKINNER. And now Lord Michael will oblige with a recitation—IF—by the inimitable Rudyard Kipling. "If you can keep your head when all about you
Are losing theirs and blaming it on you . . ."
Ladies and gentlemen, a poem to fit the place and the occasion. (*He switches off the radio.*) Lord Michael of Gas!

MICHAEL. I don't know what you think you're up to. I don't know what sort of a game you think this is. But I happen to be serious about this campaign. I marched three miles today and I attended a peaceful meeting today because every man's entitled to justice and fair play and that's what I'm campaigning for. But this—this —this fooling around, this swaggering about as if you owned the place, this isn't my idea of dignified, peaceful protest.

SKINNER. (*To LILY.*) I think he deserves to sign the distinguished visitors' book. Doesn't he?

MICHAEL. You know what you're campaigning for,

Missus. You want a decent home. And you want a better life tor your children than the life you had. But I don't know what his game is. I don't know what he wants.

SKINNER. Bunny Rabbit to romp home at twenties.

MICHAEL. Oh, as you say, he's glib alright. But if you ask me he's more at home with the hooligans, out throwing stones and burning shops! (SKINNER *stands for a moment puffing on his cigar; then begins to sing to the tune* The Wearing of the Green:—)

SKINNER. "Will you come into my parlour, said the spider to the fly." (*He deliberately stubs out his cigar on the leather desk top.*) " 'Tis the prettiest little parlour that ever you did spy." (*He prances down to the cocktail cabinet as* MICHAEL *frantically brushes the desk.*)

MICHAEL. Look, Lily, look! I told you! I told you!

SKINNER. "The way into my parlour is up a winding stair
And I have many curious things to show you when you're there."

MICHAEL. He's a vandal! He's a bloody vandal! (SKINNER *pours a drink for* LILY.)

SKINNER. Lily?

LILY. You'll have me on my ear—God bless you. (*To* MICHAEL.) Try that port wine, young fella. It's gorgeous.

SKINNER. It's sherry, Lily. Sherry, Mr. Hegarty? (MICHAEL *turns away and prepares to leave.*) Just the two of us, then, Lily. To . . . dignity.

MICHAEL. I'm going.

LILY. It's time we were all leaving. They'll be waiting for me to make the tea. (SKINNER *sits down and puts his feet up on the table.*)

SKINNER. Would anyone object if I had another cigar? (*He lights one.*)

LILY. What time is it, anyway?

MICHAEL. Coming on to five.

LILY. D'you see my wanes? If I'm not there, not one of them would lift a finger. Three years ago last May the chairman won the five pound note in the slate club raffle

and myself and Declan went on a bus run to Bundoran—
I took him with me 'cos he doesn't play about on the
street with the others, you know—and when we come
home at midnight there they all were, with faces this
length, sitting round the bare table, waiting since six
o'clock for their tea to appear!

MICHAEL. I'm away, Lily. Good luck.

LILY. Goodbye, young fella. And keep at them books.

MICHAEL. (*To* SKINNER.) Thanks for pulling me in.

SKINNER. My pleasure. And any time you're this way,
don't pass the door.

LILY. And good luck on Easter Tuesday.

MICHAEL. Thanks. Thanks. (*Before* MICHAEL *reaches
the door:*)

SKINNER. Before you go, take a look out the window.
(MICHAEL *stops, looks at* SKINNER, *then taking a chair
to stand on, looks out the window.*) Are they still there?

LILY. Is who still there?

SKINNER. The army. (*To* MICHAEL.) Have they gone
yet?

MICHAEL. The place is crawling with them! And there's
police there too!

LILY. The army's bad enough but God forgive me I
can't stand them polis.

SKINNER. If I were you I'd wait till they move.

MICHAEL. Why should I?

SKINNER. Go ahead then.

MICHAEL. Why shouldn't I?

SKINNER. Go ahead then.

MICHAEL. I've done nothing wrong.

SKINNER. How do you talk to a Boy Scout like that?

MICHAEL. I've done nothing I'm ashamed of.

SKINNER. You drank municipal whiskey. You masquer-
aded as a councillor. Theft and deception.

MICHAEL. Alright, smart alex. (*He tosses coins on the
table.*) That's for the drink—there-there-there-there. Now
give me one good reason why I can't walk straight out of

here and across that Square. One good reason—go on—
go on.

SKINNER. Because you presumed, boy. Because this is
theirs, boy, and your very presence here is a sacrilege.

MICHAEL. They don't know we're here.

SKINNER. They'll see you coming out, won't they?

MICHAEL. So they'll see me coming out and they'll
arrest me for trespassing.

SKINNER. Have a brandy on me. They'll soon shift.

MICHAEL. I certainly don't want to be arrested. But if
they want to arrest me for protesting peacefully—that's
alright—I'm prepared to be arrested.

SKINNER. They could do terrible things to you—break
your arms, burn you with cigarettes, give you injections.

MICHAEL. Gandhi showed that violence done against
peaceful protest helps your cause.

SKINNER. Or shoot you.

LILY. God forgive you, Skinner. There's no luck in talk
like that.

MICHAEL. As long as we don't react violently, as long
as we don't allow ourselves to be provoked, ultimately
we must win.

SKINNER. Do you understand Mr. Hegarty's theory,
Lily?

LILY. Youse are both away above me.

MICHAEL. I told you my name's Michael.

SKINNER. Mr. Hegarty is of the belief that if five thousand of us are demonstrating peacefully and they come
along and shoot us down, then automatically we . . . we
. . . (To MICHAEL.) Sorry, what's the theory again?

MICHAEL. You know damn well the point I'm making
and you know damn well it's true.

SKINNER. It's not, you know. But we'll discuss it some
other time. And as I said, if you're passing this way, don't
let them entertain you in the outer office. (MICHAEL goes
back to the window and looks out.)

SCENE 5-A

The lights shift to the JUDGE'S *platform.*

JUDGE. One of the most serious issues for our considera-
tion is the conflict between the testimony of the civilian
witnesses and the testimony of the security forces on the
vital question— Who fired first? Or to rephrase it— Did
the security forces initiate the shooting or did they merely
reply to it? We have heard, for example, the evidence of
Father Brosnan who attended the deceased and he insists
that none of the three was armed. And I have no doubt
that Father Brosnan told us the truth as he knew it. But
I must point out that Father Brosnan was not present
when the three emerged from the building. We have also
the evidence of the photographs taken by Mr. Montini,
the journalist, and in none of these very lucid pictures
can we see any sign whatever of weapons either in the
hands of the deceased or adjacent to their person. But
Mr. Montini tells us he didn't take the pictures until at
least three minutes after the shooting had stopped. On the
other hand, we have the sworn testimony of eight soldiers
and four policemen who claim not only to have seen
these civilian firearms but to have been fired at by them.
So at this point I wish to recall Dr. Winbourne of the
Army Forensic Department. (WINBOURNE *enters right
as a light comes up.*)

WINBOURNE. My lord.

JUDGE. Dr. Winbourne, in your earlier testimony you
mentioned paraffin tests you carried out on the deceased.
Could you explain in more detail what these tests involved?

WINBOURNE. Certainly, my lord. When a gun is fired,
the propellant gases scatter minute particles of lead in
two directions: through the muzzle and over a distance
of thirty feet in front of the gun; and through the breach.
In other words, if I fire a revolver or an automatic
weapon or a bolt-action rifle— (*He illustrates with his*

own hand.) —these lead particles will adhere to the back of this hand and between the thumb and forefinger. And a characteristic of this contamination is that there is an even-patterned distribution of these particles over the hand or clothing.

JUDGE. And the presence of this deposit is conclusive evidence of firing?

WINBOURNE. I'm a scientist, my lord. I don't know what constitutes conclusive evidence.

JUDGE. What I mean is, if these lead particles are found on a person, does that mean that that person has fired a gun?

WINBOURNE. He may have, my lord. Or he may have been contaminated by being within thirty feet of someone who has fired in his direction. Or he may have been beside someone who has fired. Or he may have been touched or handled by someone who has just fired.

JUDGE. I see. And these distinctions are of the utmost importance because on this point we must be scrupulously meticulous. Thank you, Mr. Winbourne, for explaining them so succinctly. So that, if we are to decide whether lead on a person's hand or clothing should be attributed to his having fired a weapon, we must be guided by the pattern of deposit. Is that correct?

WINBOURNE. Yes, my lord.

JUDGE. And now, if I may return to your report—your findings on the three deceased.

WINBOURNE. In the case of Fitzgerald—it's on Page four, my lord.

JUDGE. I have it, thank you.

WINBOURNE. In the case of Fitzgerald, a smear on the left hand and on the left shirt sleeve. In the case of the woman Doherty, smear marks on the right cheek and shoulder. In the case of Hegarty an even deposit on the back of the left hand and between the thumb and forefinger.

JUDGE. A patterned deposit?

WINBOURNE. An even deposit, my lord.

JUDGE. So Hegarty certainly did fire a weapon?

WINBOURNE. Let me put it this way, my lord: I don't see how he could have had these regular deposits unless he did.

JUDGE. And Fitzgerald and the woman Doherty?

WINBOURNE. They could have been smeared by Hegarty or they could have been contaminated while they were being carried away by the soldiers who shot them.

JUDGE. Or by firing themselves.

WINBOURNE. That's possible.

JUDGE. But you are certain that Hegarty at least fired?

WINBOURNE. That's what the tests indicate.

JUDGE. And you are personally convinced he did?

WINBOURNE. Yes, I think he did, my lord.

JUDGE. Thank you, Dr. Winbourne. (*The lights shift back to the Parlour as the* JUDGE *and* WINBOURNE *exit.*)

SCENE 5

SKINNER. Are you asleep, Lily?

LILY. D'you see our place? At this minute Mickey Teague, the milkman, is shouting up from the road, 'I know you're there, Lily Doherty. Come down and pay me for the six weeks you owe me.' And the chairman's sitting at the fire like a wee thin saint with his finger in his mouth and the comics up to his nose and hoping to God I'll remember to bring him home five fags. And below us Celia Cunningham's about half-full now and crying about the sweepstake ticket she bought and lost when she was fifteen. And above us Dickie Devine's groping under the bed for his trombone and he doesn't know yet that Annie pawned it on Wednesday for the wanes' bus fares and he's going to beat the tar out of her when she tells him. And down the passage aul Andy Boyle's lying in bed because he has no coat. And I'm here in the mayor's parlour, dressed up like the Duchess of Kent and drinking port wine. I'll tell you something, Skinner: it's a very unfair world. (*We hear the rumble of tanks approaching.*)

MICHAEL. There's three more tanks coming. And they seem to be putting up searchlights or something.

SKINNER. Lily.

LILY. What?

SKINNER. Why don't you ring somebody?

LILY. Who?

SKINNER. Anybody.

LILY. That young fella's out of his mind! Why in God's name would I ring somebody?

SKINNER. To wish them a happy Christmas. To use the facilities of the hotel. Just for the hell of it. Anyone in the street got a phone?

LILY. Surely. We all have phones in every room. Haaaa!

SKINNER. Where do you get your groceries?

LILY. Billy Broderick.

SKINNER. Ring him.

LILY. Sure he's across the road from me.

SKINNER. Tell him you're out of tea.

LILY. Have you no head, young fella? He'd think I couldn't face him just because I owe him fifteen pounds.

SKINNER. You must know someone with a phone.

LILY. Doctor Sweeney!

SKINNER. No doubt. Anyone working in a shop—a factory?

LILY. No.

SKINNER. A garage—a cafe—an office—an—

LILY. Beejew Betty.

SKINNER. Who?

LILY. Betty Breen. She's a cousin of the chairman. She's in the cash desk of the Beejew Cinema. We call her Beejew Betty. (SKINNER *looks up the number in the directory.* LILY *turns to* MICHAEL.) She used to let our wanes into the Saturday matinee for nothing. And then one Saturday our Tom—d'you see our Tom? Sixteen next October 23 and afeared of no man nor beast—he went up to her after the picture and told her it was the most stupidest picture he ever seen. And d'you know what? She took it personal. Niver let them in for free again. A real snob, Betty.

SKINNER. (*Dials.*) 7479336.

LILY. What are you at? Sure I seen her last Sunday week at the granny's. (SKINNER *hands her the phone.*) What will I say? What in the name of God will I say to—? (*Her accent and manner become suddenly stilted.*) Hello? Is that Miss Betty Breen? This is Mrs. Elizabeth Doherty speaking. Yes—yes—Lily. How are you keeping since we last met, Betty? No, no, he's fine, thank you, fine—the chest apart. No, I'm in good health, too, Betty, thank you. It just happened that I chanced to be with some companions near a telephone and your name come up in casual conversation, and I thought I'd say How-do-do. Yes. Yes. Well, Betty, I'll not detain you any longer, Betty. I'm sure you're busy with finance. Good-bye. No, the kiosk's still broken. I'm ringing from the mayor's parlour. (*She suddenly bangs down the receiver and covers her face with her hands.*) Jesus, young fella, I think she passed out! Oooooops!

SKINNER. That's a great start. Who else is there?

LILY. Give us a second to settle myself, will you? I'm not worth tuppence. (*She pours herself a drink.*)

SKINNER. I·love your posh accent, Lily.

MICHAEL. I want the two of you to know I object to this carry-on.

LILY. Sure it's only a bit of innocent fun, young fella. Have you no give in you at all? (*Examines bottle.*) What d'you call this port wine? I'm going to get a bottle of it next Christmas.

SKINNER. It's sherry, Lily. Who else do you know? Any friends? Relatives?

MICHAEL. You're be having exactly as they think we behave.

LILY. As who thinks?

SKINNER. Have you any uncles? Any brothers? Any sisters?

LILY. I have one sister—Eileen.

SKINNER. Is she on the phone?

LILY. She is.

SKINNER. Eileen what? What's her second name?

MICHAEL. No wonder they don't trust us. We're not worthy of trust.

LILY. You'll not get her in that book.

SKINNER. From the operator, then.

LILY. No, I'm not going to ring Eileen. She'd think something terrible had happened.

MICHAEL. And even if you have no sense of decency, at least you should know that that's stealing unless you're going to leave the money. (LILY *gives* MICHAEL *an indignant shove.*)

LILY. Lookat, young fella! I don't need your nor nobody else to tell me what's right and what's wrong. (*To* SKINNER.) Give me that. (SKINNER *hands her the phone.*) How do you get the operator?

SKINNER. Dial 100 and give your number.

LILY. I didn't say I wasn't going to leave the money, did I? I'm as well acquainted with my morals as the next. If you don't mind, I'll take my glass. Thank you. Enquiries? This is 7643225, Londonderry, Northern Ireland. I wish to make a call to Mrs. Eileen O'Donnell, 275 Riverway Drive—yes—Riverway—*Riverway*— (*The accent is dropped.*) God, are you deaf, wee girl? Riverway Drive, Brisbane, Australia. (*She hangs up.*) She'll call me back. (SKINNER *laughs and slaps the table with delight.*)

SKINNER. Lily, you're wonderful! The chairman's married to a queen. Does he deserve you?

(BRIGADIER JOHNSON-HANSBURY *enters on top of the battlements. He speaks through a loud-hailer. He is guarded by three armed soldiers.*)

BRIGADIER. Attention, please! Attention!

MICHAEL. Listen!

LILY. And when I get my breath back, I might even give a tinkle to Cousin William in the Philippines.

MICHAEL. Shut up! Listen! Listen!

BRIGADIER. This is Brigadier Johnson-Hansbury. We know exactly where you are and we know that you are armed. I advise you to surrender now before there is loss of life. So lay down your arms and proceed to the front entrance with your hands above your head. Repeat—proceed to the front entrance with your hands above your head. The Guildhall is completely surrounded. I urge you to follow this advice before there is loss of life. (*The* BRIGADIER *and the soldiers remain on the battlements. Silence.* LILY *gets to her feet.* SKINNER *gets to his feet. Pause.*)

LILY. Arms? What's he blathering about?

SKINNER. His accent's almost as posh as yours, Lily. (*Pause.*)

MICHAEL. Some bastard must have done something to rattle them—shouted something, thrown a stone, burned something—some bloody hooligan! Someone like you, Skinner! For it's bastards like you, bloody vandals, that's keeping us all on our bloody knees! (*As the lights fade we hear the Tower clock chime five.*)

END OF ACT ONE

ACT TWO

The stage is dark. In the parlour stand MICHAEL, *left,* SKINNER, *right;* LILY *is seated on the stool center. They are barely illuminated by head spots. They do not move.*

In the dark we hear the BALLADEER *whistling* Kevin Barry. *When the lights come up, we see him seated on the short section of wall left. He is very drunk.*

BALLADIER.

In Guildhall Square one sunny evening three Derry volunteers were shot.

Two were but lads and one a mother; the Saxon bullet was their lot.

They took a stand against oppression, they wanted Mother Ireland free.

Their blood now stains the Guildhall pavements; a cross stands there for all to see.

(*He stands, holding the fence for support.*)

We'll not forget that sunny evening, nor the names of those bold three

Who gave their lives for their ideal—Mother Ireland, one and free.

They join the lines of long-gone heroes, England's victims, one and all.

We have their memory still to guide us; we have their courage to recall.

(*The* BALLADEER *goes off*)

(*Lights shift to the* JUDGE *at his desk. The low lights remain on the three.*)

JUDGE. The weight of evidence presented over the past

few days seems to be directing the current of this enquiry
into the distinct areas. The first has to do with what at
first sight might appear to be mere speculation, but it
could be a very important element, I suggest, in any un-
derstanding of the entire canvass of that Saturday—and
I refer to the purpose the three had in using the Guildhall,
the municipal nerve-centre of Londonderry, as their platform of defiance. And the second area—more sensible to
corroboration or refutal, one would think—concerns the
arms the deceased were alleged to have used against the
army. And I suggest, also, that these two areas could well
be different aspects of the same question. Why the Guildhall? Counsel for the deceased pleads persuasively that in
the mêlée following the public meeting the three in their
terror sought the nearest possible cover and that cover
happened to be the Guildhall—a fortuitous choice. This
may be. But I find it difficult to accept that of all the
buildings adjacent to them they happened to choose the
one building which symbolized for them a system of government they opposed and were in fact at that time
illegally demonstrating against. And if the choice was
fortuitous, why was the building defaced? Why were its
furnishings despoiled? Why were its records defiled? Would
they have defaced a private house in the same way? I
think the answers to these questions point to one conclusion: that the deceased deliberately chose this building;
that their purpose and intent was precise and deliberate.
In other words, that their action was a carefully contrived
act of defiance against, and in incitement to others to
defy, the legitimate forces of law and order. No other
conclusion is consistent with the facts.

(*The lights go out on the* JUDGE *and as* MICHAEL *speaks
   the special on him grows brighter. When* MICHAEL,
   LILY *and* SKINNER *speak, they speak calmly, without emotion, in neutral accents.*)

MICHAEL. We came out the front door as we had been

ordered and stood on the top step with our hands above
our heads. They beamed searchlights on our faces but I
could see their outlines as they crouched beside their
tanks. I even heard the click of their rifle-bolts. But
there was no question of their shooting. I knew they
weren't going to shoot. Shooting belonged to a totally
different order of things. And then the Guildhall Square
exploded and I knew a terrible mistake had been made.
And I became very agitated, not because I was dying, but
that this terrible mistake be recognized and acknowl-
edged. My mouth kept trying to form the word mistake—
mistake—mistake. And that is how I died—in disbelief,
in astonishment, in shock. It was a foolish way for a
man to die.

(LILY *begins speaking immediately and her light grows
        brighter as* MICHAEL'S *fades.*)

   LILY. The moment we stepped outside the front door
I knew I was going to die, instinctively, the way an
animal knows. Jesus, they're going to murder me. A
second of panic—no more. Because it was succeeded,
overtaken, overwhelmed by a tidal wave of regret, not
for myself nor my family, but that life had somehow
eluded me. And now it was finished; it had all seeped
away; and I had never experienced it. And in the silence
before my body disintegrated in a purple convulsion, I
thought I glimpsed a tiny truth: that life had eluded me
because never once in my forty-three years had an experience, an event, even a small unimportant happening
been isolated and assessed and articulated. And the fact
that this, my last experience, was defined by this per-
ception, this was the culmination of sorrow. In a way I
died of grief.

(SKINNER *speaks immediately and his light grows
        brighter as* LILY'S *fades.*)

   SKINNER. A short time after I realized we were in the

mayor's parlour I knew that a price would be exacted.
And when they ordered us a second time to lay down our
arms I began to suspect what that price would be because
they leave nothing to chance and because the poor are
always overcharged. And as we stood on the Guildhall
steps, two thoughts raced through my mind: how seri-
ously they took us and how unpardonably casual we were
about them; and that to match their seriousness would
demand a total dedication, a solemnity as formal as theirs.
And then everything melted and fused in a great roaring
heat. And my last thought was: if you're going to decide
to take them on, Adrian Casimir, you've got to mend
your ways. So I died, as I lived, in defensive flippancy.

(*The lights snap back to the* JUDGE. *As he speaks the dim
lights on the three fade out completely.*)

JUDGE. We now come to the second area—were the
deceased armed? Their Counsel insists they were not.
The security forces insist they were. If they opened fire
at the army, their counsel ask with good reason, why
were there no military casualties, and even more perti-
nently, what became of their weapons. To this the army
replies that the guns were taken away by the mob which
had gathered. Counsel for the deceased strongly deny
this. They say that no civilians were allowed into the
Guildhall Square until one hour after the shooting. The
security forces say this is untrue, and point—for example
—to the priest and the newsman who where right beside
the deceased within five minutes of the shooting. So, in
view of this welter of confusion, I wish to recall the
pathologist Professor Cuppley, tomorrow morning. (*During the* JUDGE'S *speech, the three have gone back into
the same positions they were in when Act One ended.*
SKINNER *and* LILY *are still in the ceremonial robes.*
MICHAEL. *looks out the window again, then exits into
the dressing room.* LILY *looks about the dimly lighted
room and goes to the light switch up left and switches*

it on. SKINNER *gets his jacket which has been hanging on the wall sconce up center, goes to the desk, fills his pocket with cigarets from the box on the desk and lights one.*)

SCENE 6

LILY. That's better. I'm a great wan for light. The cold I don't mind but I don't like the dark. (*She takes off her robe and examines it.*) I'll tell you something, Skinner: it's a shocking sin having them lovely things lying idle in a wardrobe and them as fresh as the day they were bought. Lookat—not an elbow out of them nor nothing.

SKINNER. It has the shoulders scratched off me.

LILY. What are you wearing it for then? Give it to me, you clown you! Here's your shirt. And them gutties must be dry by now. (SKINNER *takes off the robe and gives it to* LILY. *She spreads them on the floor to fold them one at a time. He puts on the shirt.*) D'you know what that would make? A grand warm dressing-gown, wouldn't it? And that's what the chairman needs for when he be's out in the chest hospital.

SKINNER. Take it with you.

LILY. Wouldn't I look a quare sight walking along the street with this on my back! Like the time the polis came on the Boxer Brannigan driving off the fuel truck. D'you know the Boxer?

SKINNER. Th' old one-two-three-one-two-three.

LILY. And says the Boxer to them: "I was only looking for a refill for my lighter." Where's the other one? (*Robe.*)

SKINNER. Behind you. On the chair.

LILY. That young fella—what do they call him again?

SKINNER. Michael.

LILY. That's it. A grand sensible lad that.

SKINNER. Admirable.

LILY. I have a Michael. Between Declan and Gloria. His teacher says he's just throbbing with brains. Like the chairman. (SKINNER *sits left to put on his shoes.* LILY *puts the folded robes on the mayor's chair; goes to cocktail cabinet and begins dusting and putting away.*) Is the aunt alive or dead, Skinner?

SKINNER. Dead. Ten years dead.

LILY. May the Lord have mercy on her good soul. And where do you live?

SKINNER. Anywhere—everywhere. As they say—no fixed address.

LILY. And sure if you've no fixed address you can't claim no dole.

SKINNER. Right.

LILY. And how do you live?

SKINNER. On my wits.

LILY. But if anything was to happen to you—

SKINNER. If I'm sick the entire wisdom of the health authority is at my service. And should I die the welfare people would bury me in style. It's only when I'm alive and well that I'm a problem.

LILY. Isn't that peculiar? All the same, to be buried in style, that's nice.

SKINNER. Great.

LILY. And do you just knock about the town all day?

SKINNER. Sometimes I move out. To England. Scotland. The life of Riley. (LILY *is dusting the display cabinet.*)

LILY. I can't offer you no bed, Skinner, 'cos there's six in one room and seven in the other. But I could give you a bite to eat most days of the week. (*Pause.* SKINNER *suddenly pulls the ceremonial sword from his belt.*)

SKINNER. On guard! (*He fences with himself in* "mirror" *left.*)

LILY. If you're stuck.

SKINNER. Okay.

LILY. And even if I'm out working, the chairman's always there.

SKINNER. Fine.

LILY. You know the old station. That's where we live. It's a converted warehouse. Third floor up.

SKINNER. Do you like my technique?

LILY. What?

SKINNER. My swordsmanship.

LILY. Lovely.

SKINNER. How do you think I'm doing?

LILY. Great.

SKINNER. Thanks, Lily.

LILY. Who are you fighting?

SKINNER. At the moment the British army.

LILY. God help them. (LILY *is tidying the desk.* SKINNER *continues fencing a moment, stops, puts sword back in belt; crosses to her.*)

SKINNER. Lily.

LILY. What?

SKINNER. Has is anything at all to do with us?

LILY. What?

SKINNER. This marching—protesting—demonstrating?

LILY. What are you talking about, young fella?

SKINNER. Has it anything to do with you and me and him—if he only knew it?

LILY. What are you ranting about? It's for us it is. Isn't it?

SKINNER. "Doctors, plumbers, teachers, accountants, all shoulder to shoulder"—is that us?

LILY. Don't ask me nothing, young fella. I've no head. All I do is march. And if you want to know why you should be marching you ask the buck inside.

SKINNER. Why do you march?

LILY. Me?

SKINNER. Why did you march today?

LILY. Sure everybody was marching the day.

SKINNER. Why were you out?

LILY. For the same reason as everybody else.

SKINNER. Tell me your reasons.

LILY. My reasons is no different to anybody else.

SKINNER. Tell me yours.

LILY. Wan man—wan vote—that's what I want. You know—wan man—wan vote. (*She leans down to dump ashtray into wastebasket.*)

SKINNER. You got that six months ago. (*Pause. She reappears.*)

LILY. Sure I know that. Sure I know we got it.

SKINNER. That's not what you're marching for, then.

LILY. Gerrymandering—that's another thing—no more gerrymandering—that's what I want—no more gerrymandering. And civil rights for everybody—that's what I want—you know—civil rights—civil rights—that's why I march.

SKINNER. I don't believe a word of it, Lily.

LILY. I'm a liar, then?

SKINNER. And neither do you.

LILY. You're calling me a liar, is that it?

SKINNER. I'll tell you why you march.

LILY. He'll be telling me my name isn't Lily Doherty next.

SKINNER. Because you live with eleven kids and a sick husband in two rooms that aren't fit for animals. Because you exist on a state subsistence that's about enough to keep you alive but too small to fire your guts. Because you know your children are caught in the same morass. Because for the first time in your life you grumbled and someone else grumbled and someone else, and you heard each other, and became aware that there were hundreds, thousands, millions of us all over the world, and in a vague groping way you were outraged. That's what it's all about, Lily. It has nothing to do with doctors and accountants and teachers and dignity and Boy Scout honor. It's about us—the poor—the majority—stirring in our sleep. And if that's not what it's all about, then it has nothing to do with us. (LILY *gazes at him. Pause.*)

LILY. I suppose you're right. (*He switches to flippancy; jumps up on stool.*)

SKINNER. And that's why I appeal to you, when you

go into that polling station, put an X opposite my name and insure that your children too will enjoy the freedom of the city. And now I think we'll have one for the road, Lily. (*He goes to the cabinet.*) Let's walk into the future with bloodshot eyes and unsteady step. (*Pause while he rummages in cabinet.*)

LILY. Did you ever hear tell of a mongol child, Skinner?

SKINNER. Where did you hide the brandy?

LILY. I told you a lie about our Declan. That's what Declan is. He's not just shy, our Declan. He's a mongol. (*He finds the brandy decanter and pours a drink.*) And it's for him I go on all the civil rights marches. Isn't that stupid? You and him (Michael) and everybody else marching and protesting about sensible things like politics and stuff and me in the middle of you all, marching for Declan. Isn't that the stupidest thing you ever heard? Sure I could march and protest from here to Dublin and sure what good would it do Declan? Stupid and all as I am I know that much. But I still march—every Saturday —I still march. Isn't that the stupidest thing you ever heard?

SKINNER. No.

LILY. That's what the chairman said when I—you know—when I tried to tell him what I was thinking. He never talks about him; can't even look at him. And that day that's what he said, "You're a bone stupid bitch. No wonder the kid's bone stupid, too." The chairman—that's what he said. (*She stops abruptly, as if she had been interrupted.* SKINNER *goes to her and puts his glass into her hand.*) O merciful God. (*The lights shift to the* PRIEST.)

SCENE 7-A

PRIEST. At eleven o'clock tomorrow morning solemn requiem Mass will be celebrated in this church for the repose of the souls of the three people whose death has plunged this parish into a deep and numbing grief. As you are probably aware I had the privilege of administering the last rites to them and the knowledge that they didn't go unfortified to their Maker is a consolation to all of us. And it is natural that we should mourn. And it is also right and fitting that this tragic happening should make us sit back and take stock and ask ourselves the very pertinent questions: why did they die?

That there are certain imperfections in our society, this I do not deny. Nor do I deny that opportunities for gainful employment, for decent housing, for effective voting were in certain instances less than equal. And because of these imperfections, honest men and women, decent men and women came together and formed the nucleus of a peaceful, dignified movement that commanded the respect not only of this city and this country but the respect of the world. But although this movement was initially peaceful and dignified, as you are well aware certain evil elements attached themselves to it and contaminated it and ultimately poisoned it, with the result that it has long ago become an instrument for corruption.

Who are they, these evil people? I will speak and I will speak plainly. They have many titles and they have many banners; but they have one purpose and one purpose only —to deliver this Christian country into the dark dungeons of Godless communism. I don't suggest for one minute that the three people who died yesterday were part of this conspiracy, were even aware that they were victims of this conspiracy. But victims they were. And to those of you who are flirting with the doctrines of revolution, let me quote to you from that most revolutionary of doctrines—The Sermon on the Mount: "Blessed are the meek for *they* shall possess the land."

In the name of the Father, Son, and Holy Spirit.

(The lights shift back to the parlour as MICHAEL *bustles in from the dressing room.)*

SCENE 7

MICHAEL. Okay—are we all set?

SKINNER. How are the nerves now?

MICHAEL. You're not going out in that? (*Hat.*)

SKINNER. Why not?

MICHAEL. Put that hat away.

SKINNER. Would it lead to a breach of the peace?

MICHAEL. Put it back where it belongs, Skinner.

SKINNER. I'm keeping it. I think it's . . . sympathetic.
(*He adjusts the angle.*) How about that, Lily? (*He begins to sing; grabs* LILY *round the waist and turns her round a few times.*)
"Where did you get that hat,
  Where did you get that tile?
  Isn't it a hobby one and just the proper style?
  I should like to have one just the same as that . . .

LILY. Oooooops!

SKINNER.
"Where'er I go they shout 'Hello!
  Where did you get that hat?' "

LILY. You'll have me as silly as yourself, Skinner.

SKINNER. Last round before closing. Come on, gentlemen, please. Last call—last call. What's your pleasure, Mr. Hegarty?

LILY. D'you see our Tom? He found an aul saucepan on the railway lines one day last summer and put it on his head for a laugh—just like that. (SKINNER.) And didn't his head swell up with the heat and as God's my judge he was stuck in it for two days and two nights and had to sleep on the floor with the handle down a rat hole.

MICHAEL. The thing to remember is that we took part in a peaceful demonstration and if they're going to charge us, they'll have to charge 6,000 others.

SKINNER. Small Scotch?

MICHAEL. Nothing. Now, if they want to be officious, supposing they take our names and addresses, that's all they're entitled to ask for and that's all you're expected to give them. That's the law.

SKINNER. (*Toasts.*) The law. Personally speaking I'm a great man for the law myself, you know, like, there's nothing like the law.

MICHAEL. Okay Lily? And if they try to get you to make a statement, you just say you're making no statement unless your solicitor's present. /

SKINNER. My solicitor's in Bermuda. Who's yours, Lily?

LILY. Don't mention them fellas to me. They all have the wan story: You've a great case—you can't be beat. And then when you're in jail they won't let you rest till you appeal.

SKINNER. Were you ever in jail, Lily?

LILY. No. Were you?

SKINNER. Not yet.

MICHAEL. Will you listen to me!

LILY. What is it, young fella?

MICHAEL. Give them no cheek and they'll give you no trouble. We made a peaceful protest and they know that. They're not interested in people like us. It's the trouble-makers they're after.

SKINNER. They think we're armed.

MICHAEL. They know damned well we're not armed.

SKINNER. Why is the place surrounded by tanks and armoured cars?

MICHAEL. Are you ready, Missus?

SKINNER. And why are the walls lined with soldiers and police?

MICHAEL. We'll do exactly as they ask. We've nothing to hide. I'll go first. (LILY *drains her glass.*)

LILY. D'you see that sherry?

SKINNER. That's brandy.

LILY. I'd get very partial to that stuff.

MICHAEL. And if they ask you a straight question, give them a straight answer, and I promise you there'll be no trouble.

LILY. I still think them windows'd be nicer in plain glass.

MICHAEL. These (*Robes.*) were inside, weren't they? (*He takes them into the dressing room. LILY moves across the room and suddenly grabs the desk.*)

LILY. I drunk that glass far too quick. God, I come in reeling and now I'm going out reeling. D'you think would the equilibrium of my inner ear be inflamed? (*MICHAEL returns.*)

MICHAEL. Are we ready?

LILY. What time is it, young fella?

MICHAEL. Just after five.

LILY. That's grand.

MICHAEL. (*To SKINNER.*) Okay?

LILY. I'll be back in time to make the tea.

MICHAEL. We're going, Skinner. (*SKINNER slowly crosses to the mayor's seat, sits in it, and spreads himself.*)

SKINNER. I like it here. I think I'll stay.

MICHAEL. For Christ's sake!

SKINNER. You go ahead.

MICHAEL. We're all going out together.

SKINNER. Why?

MICHAEL. Because they'll think it's some sort of a trick if we split up.

SKINNER. Not if you look them clean in the eye and give them straight, honest answers.

MICHAEL. Skinner, are you coming? (*Pause.*)

SKINNER. Yes—I'm coming— (*SKINNER drains his glass and slams it down; takes off the hat and slams it down. MICHAEL turns to the "door" down right. SKINNER pulls open the desk drewer and pulls out a pile of papers, scatters them around. Talking rapidly.*) —after we've had a meeting of the corporation—then I'll go. But we can't spend the afternoon drinking civic booze and smoking civic fags and then walk off without attending to pressing civic business—no, no, no, no. That wouldn't be fair. So. Right. Have we a quorum? We have. Councillor—alderman—how are you? Take a seat. We have a short agenda today, if I remember correctly. (LILY *sits. Apologetically to* MICHAEL.)

LILY. God, I need a seat, young fella. Just for five minutes. Till my head settles. (SKINNER *continues at great speed.*)

SKINNER. You have before you an account of last week's meeting. I take it to be an accurate account of the proceedings. So may I sign it? Thank you. Thank you. And now to today's agenda. Item One. Request for annual subscription for the Society for the Prevention of Cruelty to Animals—I suggest we increase our sub to 100 pounds. Agreed? Agreed. Item Two. Derry and District Floral Society want the use of the main hall for their yearly floral display. Granted. Item Three. Tenders for painting all municipal buildings in the city—in the pink gloss?—why not. Tenders accepted.

LILY. Pink gloss? Haaaaa—that's me!

SKINNER. Item Four. Invitation to us all to attend the first night of the Amateur Opera Society's season and buffet supper afterwards. Of course we will. Love to. Item Five. Municipal grant sought by Londonderry Rugby Club to purchase extra acre of land adjacent to their present pitch. All in favor? Good. Granted. Unanimous. Fine. Item Six—

MICHAEL. Are you coming or are you not?

SKINNER. Expenses incurred by elected representatives on our recent trip to Delhi to study arterial developments from Delhi to Calcutta. I think we all benefitted from that visit, didn't we?

MICHAEL. You!

SKINNER. So I propose those expenses be passed. Seconded? Good. Good. Item Seven—

MICHAEL. When you're finished mouthing there!

SKINNER. What's wrong, Mr. Hegarty? Aren't you interested? As one of the city's 9,000 unemployed isn't it in your interest that your idleness is pursued in an environment as pleasant as possible with pets and flowers and music and gaily painted buildings? What more can you want, Mr. Hegarty?

MICHAEL. Nothing that you would want, Skinner. I can tell you that.

SKINNER. No doubt, Mr. Hegarty. But now's your opportunity to speak up, to introduce sweeping legislation, to change the face of the world. Come on, Mr. Hegarty. The voice of the fourteen percent unemployed. Speak up, man, speak up. You may never have a chance like this again.

LILY. I want the chairman to go before me so . . .

SKINNER. In a moment, Lily. Lord Michael has the floor. Well sir? (MICHAEL *is very angry but controls himself and speaks precisely.*)

MICHAEL. What I want, Skinner, what the vast majority of the people out there want, is something that a bum like you wouldn't understand: a decent job, a decent place to live, a decent town to bring up our children in— that's what we want.

LILY. Good man, young fella.

SKINNER. Go on—go on.

MICHAEL. And we want fair play, too, so that no matter what our religion is, no matter what our politics is, we have the same chances and the same opportunities as the next fella. It's not very much, Skinner, and we'll get it. Believe me, we'll get it, because it's something every man's entitled to and nothing can stop us getting what we're entitled to.

LILY. Hear—hear.

MICHAEL. And now, Skinner, you tell us what you want. You're part of the fourteen percent, too. What do you want?

(*The* BRIGADIER *enters above as before. Guarded by the three soldiers. Speaks through the loud-hailer.*)

BRIGADIER. Attention, please! Attention!
LILY. Whist! Listen!

BRIGADIER. This is Brigadier Johnson-Hansbury. I will give you five minutes more to come out. Repeat—five minutes. You will lay down your arms immediately and proceed to the front entrance with your hands above your head. The Guildhall is completely surrounded. I advise you to attempt nothing foolhardy. This is your last warning. I will wait five more minutes, commencing now. (*He goes off.* SKINNER *lifts the ceremonial sword, looks for a second at* MICHAEL, *goes to the portrait and sticks the sword into it. Turns round and smiles at* MICHAEL.)

SKINNER. It's only a picture. And a ceremonial sword.

(*The lights shift to the* JUDGE'S *area as* PROFESSOR CUP-PLEY *enters right.*)

SCENE 8-A

JUDGE. Professor Cuppley, you carried out post-mortem examinations on the three deceased.

CUPPLEY. Yes, my lord.

JUDGE. And your report states that all three were killed by SLR rifle fire.

CUPPLEY. Yes, my lord.

JUDGE. Could you tell us something about this type of weapon?

CUPPLEY. It's a high velocity rifle, using 7.62 mm ammunition; and from my point of view it's particulary untidy to work with because, if the victim has been hit several times in close proximity, it's very difficult to identify the individual injuries.

JUDGE. Could you elaborate on that?

CUPPLEY. Well, the 7.62 is a high velocity bullet which makes a small, clean entrance into the body. There's no difficulty there. But once it's inside the body, its effect is similar to a tiny explosion in that it shatters the bone and flesh tissue. And then, as it passes out of the body— at the point of exit—it makes a gaping wound and as it exits it brings particles of bone and tissue with it which make the wound even bigger.

JUDGE. I see. And your report states that the deceased died from a total of thirty-four wounds?

CUPPLEY. Forgive me correcting you, my lord, but what I said was—the second paragraph on page two—I think I pointed out that thirty-four was an approximation.

JUDGE. I see that.

CUPPLEY. Because, as I say, with the SLR it's very difficult to identify individual injuries if they're close together. But in the case of Fitzgerald there were eight distinct bullet wounds; in the case of the woman Doherty —thirteen; and in the case of Hegarty—twelve, thirteen, fourteen; I couldn't be sure.

JUDGE. I understand.

CUPPLEY. Fitzgerald's wounds were in the legs, lower abdomen, the chest and hands. Doherty's were evenly distributed over the whole body—head, back, chest, abdomen and legs. Hegarty was struck in the legs and arms —two wounds in the left leg, one in each arm; but the majority of the injuries were in the head and neck and shoulders, and the serious mutilation in such a concentrated area made precise identification almost . . . guesswork.

JUDGE. I think we have a reasonably clear picture, Professor Cuppley. Thank you.

CUPPLEY. Thank you.

(The lights shift as the JUDGE and CUPPLEY go off; They come up on DOBBS as he enters left.)

DOBBS. All over the world the gulf between the rich and the poor is widening; and to give that statement some definition let me present you with two statistics. In Latin America one percent of the population owns seventy-two percent of the land and the vast majority of the farm laborers receive no wages at all but are paid in kind. And in this country of "magnificent affluence," the richest

country in the history of civilization, twenty percent of
the population live in extreme poverty.

So the question arises: What of the future? What
solutions are the economists and politicians cooking up?
Well the answer to that is that there are about as many
solutions as there are theorists, ranging from the theory
that the poor are responsible for their own condition and
should pull themselves up by their own shoestrings to the
theory that the entire free enterprise system should be
totally restructured so that all have equal share of the
cake whether they help to bake it or not.

And until these differences are resolved, nothing signif-
icant is being done for the poor. New alignments of world
powers don't affect them. Changes of government don't
affect them. They go on as before. They become more
numerous. They become more and more estranged from
the dominant society. Their position becomes more and
more insecure. They have, in fact, no future. They have
only today. And if they fail to cope with today, the only
certainty they have is death. Good night.

(The lights come back up on the parlour. MICHAEL *and*
    LILY *are picking up papers.* SKINNER *is sitting on the
    stool down center watching them. As* MICHAEL *passes
    the portrait he reaches for the sword.)*

SCENE 8

SKINNER. *Don't touch that!* (MICHAEL *looks at him,
surprised at his intensity; then shrugs and turns away.*
SKINNER *smiles.*) Allow me my gesture. (*The chairs are
back in place; the room is as it was when they first
entered.*)

MICHAEL. That's everything. I'm going now.

LILY. We're all going, young fella. (LILY *looks around.*)
I never seen a place I went off as quick.

MICHAEL. It looks right again.

LILY. You can have it.

SKINNER. The distinguished visitors book! We haven't signed it yet! (*He and* MICHAEL *dive for the book.* MICHAEL *wins.*) Come on, Lily!

LILY. Will we? (SKINNER *snatches the book from* MICHAEL.)

SKINNER. Of course we will. Aren't you as distinguished as (*Reads.*) Admiral Howard Ericson, United States Navy.

LILY. Never heard of him. Give us the pen. What do I write?

SKINNER. Just your name. There.

LILY. Get out of my road. I need space to write. "Elizabeth M. Doherty."

SKINNER. What's the "M" for?

LILY. Marigold. What do I put down over here?

SKINNER. Where?

LILY. There. That Sunday we went to Bundoran we all signed the visitors book in the hotel we got our tea in and we all writ—you know—remarks and things, about the food and the nice, friendly waiters and all. For the food, honest to God, Skinner, it was the nicest I ever ate. I mind I writ "God bless the cook." Wasn't that good?

MICHAEL. Lily.

LILY. Coming, young fella, coming. (*To* SKINNER.) You're smart. Tell me what I'll put down there. You know—something grand.

SKINNER. "Atmosphere Victorian but cellar excellent."

LILY. Whatever that means. Sure they'd know that wouldn't be me.

SKINNER. "Decor could be improved with brass ducks and pink gloss."

LILY. Haaa. He's not going to let me forget that.

MICHAEL. Lily, please.

LILY. Hold on now—hold on a minute . . . I have it! "Looking forward to a return visit." That's it—you know —nice and ladylike.

SKINNER. Perfect. Mr. Hegarty?

MICHAEL. They won't wait any longer.

SKINNER. You're really the one should sign.

LILY. There! Not a bad fist now, is it?

SKINNER. Beautiful.

LILY. They'll think I have a quare cheek on me, won't they? What are you putting down?

SKINNER. My name.

LILY. But over at the side?

SKINNER. "Freeman of the city."

LILY. Sure that means nothing.

SKINNER. I suppose you're right, Lily.

MICHAEL. Can we go now?

LILY. God, would you give me one second, young fella? I've got to— (*She dashes into the dressing room.*)

MICHAEL. Will you for God's sake—!

LILY. (*Off.*) One second, young fella. One second.

MICHAEL. He said five minutes. What's the point in crossing them? (MICHAEL *rushes to the phone, picks up the receiver. It is dead.*)

SKINNER. Do you trust them?

MICHAEL. Do you not?

SKINNER. No.

MICHAEL. Do you trust anybody?

SKINNER. I don't trust them.

MICHAEL. Do you think they'll beat you up, Skinner?

SKINNER. Maybe.

MICHAEL. Or shoot you?

SKINNER. Maybe.

MICHAEL. You really think they'd shoot you? You really do?

SKINNER. Yes. They're stupid enough. But as long as they've only got people like you to handle, they can afford to be. (LILY *returns.*)

LILY. That's better. Are we all ready?

MICHAEL. Come on.

LILY. You know where I live, young fella. Don't forget to bring Norah over to see us.

MICHAEL. Promise.

LILY. And you'll call in any time you want a bite to eat.

SKINNER. I'll be there on the stroke of one every day.

LILY. You needn't bother your head. Just when you're stuck. (*To Sir Joshua.*) Goodbye, Mister.

MICHAEL. I'll go in front.

LILY. Goodbye, young fella.

MICHAEL. Good luck, Lily.

SKINNER. Shouldn't we go out singing "We shall overcome"?

MICHAEL. I'm warning you, Skinner!

SKINNER. Do you not trust them?

LILY. Lord, I enjoyed that. The talk was good. Wasn't the talk good, Skinner? (MICHAEL *goes up left and switches off the lights.* SKINNER *nods.*) Good luck, son.

SKINNER. Good luck, Lily. (*Pause. They are about to shake hands. Then* SKINNER *leans forward to kiss her on the forehead.*)

LILY. Jesus, not since the chairman was coorting me, have I . . . (*Pause. Then to shatter the moment,* SKINNER *begins to sing softly.* LILY *hesitates a moment. Then she takes his offered arm and joins him; they do a couple of steps and a turn.*)

SKINNER. "As I walked along the Bois de Boulogne with an independent air, You could hear the girls declare he must be a millionaire."

MICHAEL. For Christ's sake!

LILY. Come on! Come on! Get to hell out of this damned place! I hated it from the first moment I clapped eyes on it! (MICHAEL *raises his hands over his head.* LILY *looks at him, amazed; turns to* SKINNER *for confirmation. He grabs the hat, slaps it on his head and thrusts his hands in the air.* LILY *slowly complies. As* MICHAEL *turns downstage to go out the "door" to the corridor, the stage goes black.*)

(*In the darkness, the auditorium is filled with thundering, triumphant organ music on open diapason. It is sustained for about 5 seconds and then faded to background as* LIAM O'KELLY *of Telefís Éireann enters on the battlements with a microphone in one hand and an umbrella in the other. He talks into the microphone in soft reverential tones.*)

O'KELLY. I am standing just outside the Long Tower church. And now the solemn requiem Mass, concelebrated by the four Northern bishops is at an end, and the organ is playing Bach's most beautiful, most triumphant and in a curious way most appropriate *Prelude and Fugue,* Number 552. And the clouds that have overcast this bitterly cold and windswept city of Derry this February morning can contain themselves no longer, and an icy rain is spilling down on all those thousands of mourners who couldn't get into the church and who have been waiting here in silent tribute along these narrow ghetto streets. But despite the rain, no one is moving. They still stand, as they have stood for the past two hours, their patient, drawn faces towards the church door; and as one watches them, one wonders will this enormous grief ever pass, so deeply has it furrowed the mind of this ancient, noble, suffering city of Saint Colmcille.

(During this, a pale, ghostly light has come up showing the three spaced across the stage with their hands above their heads.)

And now the church doors are open and the first of the cortege emerges. This is surely the most impressive gathering of church and state dignitaries that this humble parish of the Long Tower has ever seen. There is the Cardinal Primate, his head stooped, looking grave and weary; and indeed he must be weary because he flew in from Rome only this morning in order to be here today. And beside him I see Colonel Foley who is representing the President. And immediately behind them are the members of the hierarchy and the spiritual leaders of

every order and community in the country. And now the
Prime Minister, bare-headed, gently refusing an umbrella
being offered by one of the stewards; and flanking him
are the leaders of the two main opposition parties. Indeed
I understand that the entire Dail and Senate are here
today. And if one were to search for a word that would
best describe the atmosphere here today, the tenor of the
proceedings, the attitude of the ordinary people, I think
the word would be dignified.

(*The three begin to move slowly forward until they are
standing in the spots where we first saw their corpses
at the beginning.*)

And now the first of the coffins. And all around me
the men are removing their caps and some are kneeling
on the wet pavements. This is the remains of Michael
Joseph Hegarty. And immediately behind it the coffin
of Elizabeth Doherty, mother of eleven children. And
lastly the remains of Adrian Fitzmaurice—I beg your
pardon—Adrian Fitzgerald, and this coffin is being carried
by the Red Cross volunteers. And as the cortege passes
me, the thousands on the footpaths move gently forward
on to the road and take their place quietly among the
mourners. I now hand you over to our unit in the
cemetery.

(*The music swells for perhaps 5 seconds. O'KELLY makes
his way off stage. Then, suddenly, the music stops
and the lights shift to the JUDGE's platform. Two
soldiers stand at attention below him. MICHAEL,
LILY, and SKINNER stand motionless.*)

JUDGE. In summary my conclusions are as follows:
One. There would have been no deaths in Londonderry
on February 10 had the ban on the march and the meeting been respected, and had the speakers on the platform

not incited the mob to such a fever that a clash between the security forces and the demonstrators was almost inevitable.

Two. There is no evidence to support the accusation that the security forces acted without restraint or that their arrest force behaved punitively.

Three. There is no reason to suppose that the soldiers would have opened fire if they had not been fired on first.

Four. I must accept the evidence of eye-witnesses and various technical experts that the three deceased were armed when they emerged from the Guildhall, and that two of them at least—Hegarty and the women Doherty—used their arms. Consequently it was impossible to effect an arrest operation.

The detailed findings of this tribunal I will now pass on to the appropriate authorities. (*The* JUDGE *collects his notes and steps down from his platform. The two soldiers move so that one leads the* JUDGE, *the other follows. A* PHOTOGRAPHER *and a* REPORTER *have emerged from the shadows left. The* PHOTOGRAPHER *takes a flash picture of the* JUDGE *as he crosses center. The* JUDGE *ignores him. The* REPORTER *tries to get a statement; the* JUDGE *brushes past him and exits up left, accompanied by the soldiers. The only light is the three pools.*)

(*The* REPORTER *and* PHOTOGRAPHER *confer for a moment down center, paying no attention to the three. The* PHOTOGRAPHER *exits up left. The* REPORTER *grinds out a cigaret on the floor and follows.* MICHAEL, LILY *and* SKINNER *stand motionless. Pause. Silence for 15 seconds. Then the air is filled with a 15 second burst of automatic fire and the spotlights snap on. The gunfire stops. The three stand as before, staring out, their hands above their heads. Blackout.*)

THE END

FURNITURE

large desk, leather top
high backed chair behind desk
2 side chairs
upholstered bench
rolling cocktail cabinet with brandy, whiskey, port, sherry,
    2 snifters, 1 wine, 2 highball glasses, bar towel
radiogram, record player, flat top
British flag with stand
display case containing: pistol, sword, dressing, descriptive tags
portrait "Sir Joshua" (rigged to be stabbed each performance)
swivel chair (Judge's)
small desk (Judge's) with papers, files, etc.
carpet

SET PROPS

loud hailer
2 walkie talkies
portable T.V. Camera, back pack
vase of flowers on top of radiogram
silver desk set
visitor's book
brass plaque (for window)
brass plaque (for portrait)
cigar box with cigars
desk phone
Northern Ireland phone book
ash tray
cigarette box with cigarettes
in desk drawer—papers, memos, files, etc.
lighter on desk
1 rifle
cushion in Mayor's chair
wastepaper basket—under desk
dressing: rubble, sandbags

PERSONAL PROPS

packet cigarettes—Skinner
press camera with strobe—Photographer
2 wrist watches—Michael, Dobbs
money (paper and coin)—Michael
pocket knife—Skinner
4 handkerchiefs—Priest, Lily, Michael, Skinner

LIGHT CUES

Cue No.	Page No.	Description
1	9	forestage up (Bodies)
2	9	Constable and Judge
3	11	lights down except Judge
4	12	lights up D. C. for Dobbs (enter R.)
5	14	out on Dobbs; up for Lily, Michael, Skinner entrance
6	19	out in parlour; up on 2 soldiers L. & R.
7	20	out on Soldiers; up on O'Kelly top of wall
8	21	out on O'Kelly; up on Balladier & Cronies, L. & R.
9	21	out on Singer; up on parlour
10	28	out in parlour; up on Priest—top U. C.
11	29	B.O. (Voices)
12	29	up D. R. and D. L. for "Press Conference"
13	31	out D. R. and D. L.; up in parlour
14	36	out in parlour
15	36	up on Judge and Brigadier
16	38	out on Judge and Brigadier; up on Dobbs S. R.
17	39	out on Dobbs; up in parlour
18	46	out in parlour; up on Judge
19	46	up on Winbourne (D. R. C.)
20	48	out on Judge/Winbourne; up in parlour
21	51	sneak up for Brigadier top of wall
22	52	B.O. (End Act One)
23	53	up on Balladier L. C.
24	53	out on Balladier; up on Judge
25	54	up on Michael—parlour L.
26	54	out on Michael, up on Lily parlour D. C.
27	56	out on Lily; up on Skinner parlour R.
28	56	out on Skinner
29	56	out on Judge; up in parlour
30	56	practical bump up—parlour
31	61	out in parlour; up on Priest top U. C
32	62	out on Priest; up in parlour
33	67	sneak up for Brigadier top of wall

LIGHT CUES

Cue No.	Page No.	Description
34	68	out on parlour; up on Judge & Cuppley D.R.C.
35	69	out on Judge & Cuppley; up on Dobbs D. L. C.
36	70	out on Dobbs; up in parlour
37	73	practical dump down—parlour
38	74	up on forestage for O'Kelly
39	75	end O'Kelly, Judge on
40	76	exit Judge, etc.
41	76	B.O. (End Act Two)

SOUND CUES

Cue No.	Page No.	Description
1	9	tower chimes/ambulance siren
2	13	civil rights meeting/Woman's voice over
3	13	approach of tanks
4	13	Woman's speech from script
5	14	rubber bullets, gas cannisters, followed by screaming, etc.
6	14	burst of gunfire
7	14	shots, followed by screaming/tanks
7A	21	accordion
8	29	voices-recorded dialogue from script
9	35	radio—waltz
10	36	radio out
11	40	radio—"Lily of Laguna" & "Monte Carlo"
12	42	radio out
13	49	tanks approaching
14	51	loud hailer (live)
15	52	end act—tower chimes
16	68	loud hailer (as before)
17	73	organ music
18	75	level change
19	76	firing

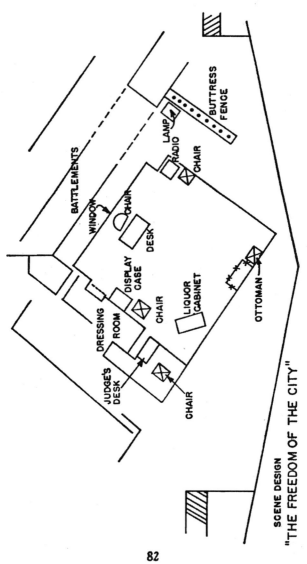

BATTLEMENTS

WINDOW

CHAIR

DESK

DISPLAY
CASE

CHAIR

DRESSING
ROOM

JUDGE'S
DESK

CHAIR

LIQUOR
CABINET

OTTOMAN

LAMP

RADIO

CHAIR

BUTTRESS
FENCE

82

SCENE DESIGN
"THE FREEDOM OF THE CITY"

MUSIC USE NOTE

Licensees are solely responsible for obtaining formal written permission from copyright owners to use copyrighted music in the performance of this play and are strongly cautioned to do so. If no such permission is obtained by the licensee, then the licensee must use only original music that the licensee owns and controls. Licensees are solely responsible and liable for all music clearances and shall indemnify the copyright owners of the play(s) and their licensing agent, Samuel French, against any costs, expenses, losses and liabilities arising from the use of music by licensees. Please contact the appropriate music licensing authority in your territory for the rights to any incidental music.

IMPORTANT BILLING AND CREDIT REQUIREMENTS

If you have obtained performance rights to this title, please refer to your licensing agreement for important billing and credit requirements.